THE HUNTER'S BETRAYAL

GUARDIANS OF SANCTUARY BOOK FOUR

TL SHIVELY

Edited by: Partners In Crime Book Services
Cover design by: Karima Creations
Formatting by: Rebecca Poole

ACKNOWLEDGMENTS

Writing inspiration comes from all around me, from friends, to family and even coworkers. The best thing is when some of them not only agree to be part of my story but also ask to be part of my Guardians' world. From several of the Alaskan Guardians with the pixie princess Darrold to the Rogue Hunters as well as the Game Master and creators of Crystal Paladins, thank you all for being a part of my world.

When doing research, I asked some readers for some ideas, Lisa, Jerry and Lily all came forward with some interesting stories and a few made it into the book. Thank you as well for giving me more inspiration.

I have been lucky to have the best support in family, friends and young readers who have made all this worthwhile. From a young lady who is as inspiring as she is creative to a young man whose grandmother met me at one of my very first book signings and since then she has made sure to purchase every book as they come out for her grandson, whose birthday is in June and the reason I had to make sure this book was published before then. HAPPY BIRTHDAY JACOB!

GLOSSARY

- Aerodisk - Crystal disk designed to float anyone or anything close to it, used by a remote
- Arions - The inhabitants of Sanctuary
- Blood Crystals - The first crystals that were discovered, they were blood-red in color
- Capture Nets - Cylindrical metal w/crystal buttons and a crystal net inside that once released captures a shadow, then transports it.
- Chenra - A magical metal used by Serdita and her sister Soliel to make music
- Command Center - The military establishment that resides in the mountains that protects Sanctuary
- Crim - Crystals used to enhance the power of an Arion, only the Guardians are able to use their powers without a Crim
- Crystal Bombs - Crystals used in the battle with the Shadows that explode in a burst of light
- Crystal Essence - The powder from crystals that is highly unstable

- Crystal Stocks - A crystal and metal belt used to contain an individual, used by a remote
- Healers - Arions who use the crystals to heal or do damage control such as adjust someone's memory
- Hovercrafts - Motorcycles with hover disks instead of wheels.
- Hoverlifters - Forklifts with hover disks instead of wheels.
- Illusion Crystals - Crystals used to create illusions to help the Arions keep the knowledge of their existence from the world
- Leaders - A group that run the Sanctuary, it should be noted that Arions have never seen any of them
- Liberator Crystal - A parent crystal used for Libertor Crims and Liberator bombs. Forged from Savanna's powers it heals Shadows that were created from humans or mythicals.
- Magine - A shadow creature created by the Shadow Master, Crims don't affect this creature, only the Guardians can stop it
- Memory Crims - Crystals used in altering someone's memory
- Mythrian Metal - A special metal used in the creation of Crims
- Normies - Mortals who know nothing of the Sanctuary
- Parent Crystals - Large Crystals that are used to give the crystal Crims their power
- Power Ball - A crystal ball used in training one's powers
- Productive Crims - Crystals used in daily life around the Command Center powering computers, opening doors and more
- Rotary - The magical Crim bracelet that was

designanted as unstable but now resides on Telara's wrist

- Shadow Detector - Crystal disk designed to detect Shadows in the area
- Shadow Generals - More human looking than the minions and bigger in size, they command the minions and only battle when needed by the shadow master
- Shadow Master - The being that controls all the shadows
- Shadow Minions - The lowest ranking of Shadows and also most common, if you were playing chess these would be considered the pawns
- Shadows - Creatures made of shadows commanded by the Shadow Master
- Stargazer - A black slim box resembling a small laptop covered with strange symbols that only I.Q. is able to understand
- Static Room - Room in the Bungalow where the Guardians could relax with their powers
- The Crystal Paladins - A popular game that can be played on a console or with cards.
- Tracker Signals - A crystal and metal disk that can be used to help others find you, once you activate you are the only one able to deactivate it

CHARACTER GUIDE
(IN ORDER OF APPEARANCE)

- Lucius - Caretaker of Sanctuary; first appearance in The Secret Sanctuary
- Mica - Earth Paladin; first appearance in The Battle of Sleeping Lady
- Kull - Fire Paladin; first appearance in The Town That Time Forgot
- Serdita - Singer in Silest's tavern who is more than she appears; first appearance in The Secret Sanctuary
- Drago - The best Game Master of the popular game Crystal Paladins; debut appearance
- Pam - Leader of the Alpha faction at Sanctuary; first appearance in The Secret Sanctuary
- Telara - Guardian of the Mind and unspoken leader; first appearance in The Secret Sanctuary
- Chad - Guardian of Ice; first appearance in The Secret Sanctuary
- Chance - Guardian of water; first appearance in The Secret Sanctuary
- Cole - Guardian of fire; first appearance in The Secret Sanctuary

- I.Q. (Maximillian) - Guardian of electricity; first appearance in The Secret Sanctuary
- Vanna (Savanna) - Guardian of earth; first appearance in The Secret Sanctuary
- Donny - Alpha enforcer at Sanctuary; first appearance The Secret Sanctuary
- Zeke - Leader of the Delta faction and history buff of Sanctuary; first appearance The Town That Time Forgot
- Gabe - Leader of the Theta faction; first appearance The Secret Sanctuary
- Chez - Beat enforcer from Sanctuary; first appearance The Secret Sanctuary
- Brian - One of the creators of the Crystal Paladins; debut appearance
- Levi - The second half of the creators of the Crystal Paladins; debut appearance
- Aurelius - Rogue Hunter; debut appearance
- Trevor - Rogue Hunter enforcer; debut appearance
- Wes - Alaskan Arion; first appearance The Battle of Sleeping Lady
- Paul - Alaskan Arion; first appearance The Battle of Sleeping Lady
- Jayne - Alaskan Arion; first appearance The Battle of Sleeping Lady
- Lucy - Rogue Hunter Admin; debut appearance
- Jeff - Rogue Hunter second-in-command; debut appearance
- Travis - Rogue Hunter; debut appearance
- Jessie - Rogue Hunter; debut appearance
- Mark - Rogue Hunter Liaison; debut appearance
- James - Rogue Hunter; debut appearance
- Zach - No one knows who this person is except that he has only shown himself to Telara, it is believed he

is a ghost of a past Guardian; first appearance The Secret Sanctuary
- Spencer - Rogue Hunter; debut appearance
- Leroy - Gnome; debut appearance
- Flint - Rogue Hunter who went Rogue; debut appearance
- Kashan - Drago best friend and fellow Game Master; debut appearance
- Tobias - Leader of the Omega faction at Sanctuary; first appearance The Secret Sanctuary
- Carmen - Leader of the Beta faction at Sanctuary; first appearance The Secret Sanctuary
- Claw - Leader of the Gamma faction at Sanctuary; first appearance The Secret Sanctuary
- Gage - Second-in-command of the Alpha faction at Sanctuary; first appearance The Secret Sanctuary

1

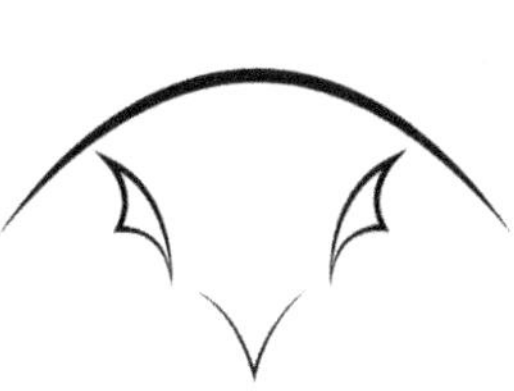

LUCIUS LOOKED over at Mica and Kull, who sat in the leather chairs in his office. Mica drank her tea with the posture of a royal holding court while Kull sat staring at Lucius through brooding eyes while he lounged in the other chair, his legs stretched out before him and crossed at the ankles. They were two completely different personalities, but regardless of those differences they were not only comrades but best of friends. All of the Paladins were. Lucius gave an inner sigh at the direction of his thoughts.

He was the caretaker of Sanctuary. He helped guide the Guardians who were destined to battle the Shadow Master's evil creation, the Magine. Since the Greek Gods and Goddesses went silent, that was his duty, to keep peace between the Greek deities and the Arions that lived in Sanctuary. He guided the Guardians, sent them to battle the Magine and waited for the next set of Guardians.

Each time the cycle was the same, the only thing that kept him sane in all these years was the prophecy that spoke of the seventh set of Guardians that would finally break the cycle and free the Paladins. Kull was freed last year when the Guardians traveled to the town of Lapros that was cursed by the Gods, stuck in time with Kull cursed as a dragon. The Guardians liberated him, therefore freeing the townsfolk and Kull's true love from the curse and allowing them to finally be at peace in death.

At the beginning of summer, the Guardians traveled to Alaska where they released Mica from her curse as a tree, planted in the ground at the home of the pixie princess, Darrold. They still had no clue who cursed her or why, but he was thankful she was here. She joined the Guardians in thwarting one of the Shadow Master's followers from awaking the Sleeping Lady, a giantess in Alaska that has slept for many years waiting for her true love to return, not knowing that her true love perished long ago, something she could never know.

"So, you going to fill us in, Caretaker?" Kull's voice rumbled with irritation, which pulled Lucius from his musings and brought a smile to his face. Much to Kull's annoyance.

"Sorry, Kull." Lucius tried to sound sincere but the smile he couldn't hide had Kull glaring at him while Mica gave him a look that spoke her disbelief at his words. "I have missed you both, it still feels surreal that you are here finally."

"But we are not complete, we still have missing pieces," Mica reminded him gently.

"Yes." Lucius nodded in acknowledgment, his voice full of regret. "I know you have a lot of questions," he gave a wry grin looking at Kull, "and a lot of complaints."

Kull raised a brow at that. "With reasons."

Lucius shrugged. "I will tell you what I know but understand this, there is much I don't know. I have many unanswered questions as well."

Kull gave him a skeptical look. "Since when have you settled for being in the dark on anything, Caretaker?"

"Kull, hush," Mica reprimanded him, her delicate features

marred by the frown she bestowed on Kull, who paid her no mind.

"That's all right, Mica," Lucius gave her an appreciative smile. "He's right," Kull grunted as if to say he didn't need Lucius to tell him that. "I don't like being in the dark, but in this case, I didn't have any choice in the matter."

Mica turned her bemused gaze upon him. "Please explain, Lucius."

"Larsa came to this realm to find the Crystal Heart after we defeated her tyrannical reign in our own realm," Lucius spoke only to be interrupted by Kull.

"We know this alread- Ouch!" Kull glared at Mica and her disappearing vine. "Woman, don't make me torch your precious plants." His hand started to glow red with small flames.

An elegant brow slowly rose at his words, then her eyes narrowed at the flames in his hand, effectively silencing him like no other could. "Please continue Lucius, and we will try to show some respect and not interrupt again." Her words earned her a dirty look but she ignored Kull as she waited for Lucius to continue.

"You'll have to excuse my trip down memory lane." Lucius looked over at Kull. "I've had no one to speak of home with in all these years. Since we traveled from our realm to this one and I lost the only family I knew."

"What about Serdita and her siblings?" Kull crossed his arms.

"Have you ever tried having an actual conversation with any of them?" Lucius asked him.

Kull shrugged. "Very few Melonians actually know how to have a conversation that doesn't leave you with more questions than you started with."

"Kull," Mica protested. "Marsella is a Melonian."

"I said *very few*," he pointed out. "Marsella is one of the few Melonians I can stand."

"He isn't far from being right," Lucius spoke up, earning him a reproving look from Mica. "I'm sorry Mica, but after spending all these years trying to get an answer from Serdita and her siblings, I can understand Kull's feelings and many others' from our home."

Mica sighed. "That is their way, they cannot help it. They can't!" Her volume rose slightly when Kull snorted at her words. "Melonians are the visionaries of our realm, the seers, prophets, artists and entertainers."

Mica stopped and stared at Lucius silently, whatever had caused her pause in her tirade, Lucius knew he wasn't going to like it. The smirk Kull sent his way said that he knew it as well.

"I wonder if you asked the Guardians if they would say the same about you." Mica was the sweetest of the Paladins but never one to mince words. Especially when she was irritated.

"I'm sure they would, Mica, and we have Serdita and her family to thank for that." Lucius sighed when Mica looked down at her hands; he hadn't meant to snap at her. The temperature in the room rose slightly, showing that Kull wasn't happy about Mica being upset either. "I'm sorry, Mica. This frustrates me as much as it does everyone else."

"I understand, Lucius," Mica spoke softly. "Please continue."

"You know how Larsa had convinced Zeus to help her in her quest for the Crystal Heart that she believed would restore her loss of power." Lucius spoke and Kull snorted.

"Didn't take much to convince him, a promise of more power with no proof."

Mica shrugged, "Your mother may have been evil incarnate but she still had the good looks and we know well the wandering eyes of the Greek Deities." Then she gasped and looked up at Lucius, her eyes of remorse over her words.

Lucius smiled at her. "Marsella told me you knew about my parentage before she disappeared. I've made peace with the fact that my mother wasn't the woman I thought she was." A sigh escaped him. "I just wish my father or myself had seen her true self before she was able to gain the power she always coveted, maybe he would still be alive."

"No one knows when she started the coup," Mica gently informed him.

"As encompassing as her grab for absolute power was, we believe that this was something that was started long before Larsa was even born."

Lucius nodded at Kull. "Yes, I know."

"So enough of the 'poor me' talk and let's get on with the fact that your mother used her wiles on Zeus and got us all cursed," Kull told him, staring at him.

"Kull!" Mica turned around to give him one of her disproving looks but Lucius laughed, which probably was the only thing that saved Kull from another headache.

"It's all right, Mica. Kull is right, now is not the time for self-pity." The two surprised faces had him grinning, he couldn't remember when the last time was when he smiled as much as he has been doing since both Kull and Mica have come back into his life. But Mica was right, they were still missing family.

"As I said, I don't have all the answers but I'm willing to tell you both what I know." Lucius leaned forward, putting his clasped hands on his desk. "But you will have to put up with listening to some reruns." Both looked at him funny, making him realize how much the influence these Guardians had on him. He gave a low laugh. "Sorry. After coming to this realm and finally finding my mother, we fought her and thought we had defeated her."

"We were going to leave but you voted to stay," Mica remembered.

Lucius nodded. "I knew my mother too well, knew she always had a backup plan."

"Zeus," Kull growled. "He hid her when I discovered what he had done. He had my town cursed and turned me into a dragon so I couldn't tell anyone what he had done."

Lucius nodded. "He did, and we didn't know that because you disappeared. When we went to Lapros, the town was gone."

Kull looked at him, his eyes bright with emotion. "The twins?"

Lucius gave a nod. "We found them and brought them home to Sanctuary." Kull's eyes narrowed at Lucius, as if he sensed there was more to the caretaker's words but Mica started speaking.

"Marsella and Kaze sent us to look for you, we all went in different directions, leaving our children back at the original Sanctuary with Marsella, Kaze and Lucius," Mica told him in her calm voice.

"Only Luce and Dreven returned." Lucius looked at Mica. "We had no answers from any of the others, we didn't know what happened."

Mica shook her head slowly at him. "If you are wanting an answer from me, then I am sorry, I do not have one for you. I do not know what happened to me. All I can remember is leaving Greece looking for Kull and Safron, then … nothing."

"What happened after Luce and Dreven returned?" Kull asked when they became silent.

"That was when we realized we were being taken out one by one," Lucius spoke, his words and face somber. "We confronted Zeus about protecting Larsa, not only did he deny it but he accused us of trying to undermine his power and overthrow the Gods by our lies. We ended up spending more time guarding the children and ourselves from the malice of the Greek Deities as well as protecting the people of Greece who stood by our side. We weren't able to continue looking for our missing comrades."

Kull's face hardened with his words while Mica gave him an encouraging smile. But neither spoke, not wanting to interrupt Lucius.

"Even staying close, they still managed to take out Luce and Dreven." Lucius felt the weight of their loss still but somehow being able to tell the story also lifted a weight he had carried around for so long. "The children grew up, fell in love and had children of their own, but still we had no answer on what had happened to any of you. We knew that the Gods had a hand in your disappearances, but no proof and no answers."

He looked over to his bookshelf where the pictures of all past Guardians sat, behind them were the drawings of the Paladins, of his friends that he missed so much.

"What happened to Marsella and Kaze?" Mica asked him, bringing his thoughts back to the present.

"I want to know what Hades' role is in all this." Kull spoke in his gruff voice. "Thought Zeus was Larsa's savior."

It hurt Lucius to remember what happened to Marsella and Kaze, he wasn't sure he had come to terms with what happened. Kull's interruption gave him the reprieve he wasn't even aware he wanted.

"After the Gods started the prophecy, Zeus decreed that no more would the Gods and Goddesses walk amongst the mortals," Lucius spoke, his chest tight with his words as she thought back to that day. "He chose Hades as his messenger; it was Hades who spoke for Zeus when he brokered the deal between us and the Gods."

"The deal that kept sending our kids to their deaths?" Mica frowned.

"Sadly, yes." Lucius breathed in deep. "We were told the children of the Paladins were the Guardians and that the Guardians were the only ones who could keep her asleep until it was time for the final battle." Lucius closed his eyes with a grimace of pain. "We didn't understand what that meant until it was too late, the cycle had already started."

"What cycle?" Kull leaned forward. "Does this cycle have to do with the prophecy?"

Lucius nodded. "With the death of the first Guardian it set the prophecy into motion, one that couldn't be stopped. Larsa would awaken and unless the Guardians stopped her, she would set forth an endless cycle of destruction and despair that couldn't be stopped. I didn't realize the cost."

"Cost?" Mica tilted her head in curiosity.

"In each battle, the Guardians would fall and, in their deaths, Larsa would once again slumber." Lucius swallowed hard. "Each battle, I sent your children to their deaths. If I knew what would happen, I would never have agreed."

"Why haven't you attempted to stop it?" Kull asked him, his brow furrowed in irritation.

"Because if he had stopped it, the prophecy would fail and darkness would descend on this realm and all would be lost, including the Paladins."

Serdita's voice came from the doorway. Turning, they saw her standing there, smiling sweetly at them, her blond hair falling over her shoulders with her shimmering pink gown flowing around her. Her Chenras were ever present, although they were silent but as always around her wrist as she stood there.

"You!" Kull's voice was no more than a growl as he glared at her while she barely acknowledged his existence. "You're why our children and their children are being led to their deaths like lambs to a slaughter?"

"No, that would be Larsa," Serdita informed him without looking his way, her gaze instead on the cupboard where the dragons sat just as they were before, the white one glowing while the black one sat silent. "The Guardians can't defeat her alone; they need the Paladins and the Paladins need the Guardians."

"So, what is Hades' role in this prophecy?" Mica asked her.

Serdita gave a shrug of her shoulder, the golden adornments on her shoulder making a twinkling sound with her movement. "I only know my role and what I am to tell you."

"He seems to have a vested interest in all this," Kull spoke, his aggravation showing, whether it was with Serdita practically ignoring him or what she was saying, but it was there.

Serdita finally looked at him and nodded, "That is his story to tell, not mine. For now, you need to know that the original prophecy is still in play."

"Original?" Mica's voice showed the concern shining in her eyes. "You mean there is more?"

"There is always more," Serdita informed her. "With each action, another prophecy emerges and sometimes these actions not only upset the original prophecy but can either change or destroy it. That hasn't happened with the original prophecy." Then she looked over at Lucius. "And as much as someone has tried to circumvent this one, it is amazing it is still intact."

"Why, Lucius?" Mica asked him.

"I was tired of sending your children to their deaths."

"Oh Lucius." Mica, ever the gentle one, looked at him with compassion.

"The final battle will take place; the Paladins and the Guardians will stand side by side when they battle Larsa," Serdita told them.

"Do you know where they are?" Kull demanded more than requested.

Serdita shrugged before she turned around and walked out the door into the hallway. Kull jumped up and went after her, only to stop in the doorway looking down the empty hallway, then turned back to them, looking perplexed. "What was that?"

"Welcome to my world." Lucius shrugged. "She only gives me a bit of information at a time, enough so I follow the prophecy but not enough so I can change it to save the Guardians."

"Do you know where the others are? Why don't we go find them so that we can go take care of Larsa and her darkness?" Kull looked ready to do just that.

Lucius gave a solemn shake of his head. "I said the same thing to Serdita and she made sure to tell me another part of the prophecy, only so I will know the futility of attempting to do just that."

Mica looked curious, "What was it?"

"That only the Guardians can wake the Paladins, blood of my blood." Lucius still wore the same solemn expression.

"Too damn many prophecies and riddles, not enough answers." Kull's brow furrowed. When Lucius opened his mouth Kull snapped, "I know, it's the Melonian way. Doesn't mean it's right, there has to be a way to get them to tell us what we need to know."

"Even with the beatings my mother gave the seer she held prisoner, the seer never wavered." Lucius looked at Kull as he spoke.

"Did anyone ever find out the prophecy that sent your mother to this realm?" Mica questioned.

Lucius looked over at her, "No, and she killed her seer so no one would be able to find out. What I do know is that she wants the Crystal Heart, that it's powerful and Telara is in possession of it." The last was spoken with a heavy tone, telling of his concern.

"Where are the Guardians now? Why aren't they trying to search out the rest of our Paladins?" Kull asked.

"They aren't searching for the others because I wasn't allowed to tell them about that part of the prophecy." Lucius gave a low snort. "I'm barely able to tell them anything but the fictional story I have told every set of Guardians."

"So, where are they?" Kull asked him again.

"I believe they and some of the other Arions are going to something they call a … Crystal-Con," Lucius told him.

"Crystal-Con? Is this some sort of training?" Kull crossed his arms as he asked that question.

The first time Lucius actually felt like smiling, although he tried to bite back the grin. "I believe it's a place for games and dressing up as fictional characters."

"Games? Dressing up?" Kull's voice raised in volume. "We have a battle that needs them and you let them go play unaccompanied? This isn't the time for them to play, they're needed to find the others so we can take down Larsa once and for all."

"They can't spend all their time training, Kull," Mica told him, her eyes daring him to argue with her.

"Besides, who says they're not being accompanied?" Lucius spoke up before a battle could take place in his office. "They know nothing of the prophecy and they deserve the break."

Kull glowered at Lucius then turned and stormed out of the office.

2

"THERE'S ONLY one rule in this game!" The guy in the center of the room on stage, with dark skin glimmering with perspiration, standing at least six foot tall in a dark cloak, spoke into the microphone as his voice boomed all around them. "Don't die!"

The cheers around them deafened them with their chants.

"Drago! Drago! Drago!"

"Who is that?" Pam looked at Telara, who winced at the yelling going on around them.

"That is the best Game Master ever." Chad grinned at them, his hazel eyes shining with excitement, his brown hair curling at the nape of his neck. The length of his hair was the only difference you could see between him and his twin brother, Chance, whose full attention was on the center stage.

"Game Master?" Pam gave him a weird look, moving her dark hair behind her ear, trying not to flinch with the volume of the room. Growing up in Sanctuary and leading the Alpha faction there must have not left her much time for fun and games.

"The Crystal Paladins," Cole told her, grinning like the

Cheshire Cat. "The only game worth playing." In his hands were the cards he brought with him, cards from the card game him, Chad and I.Q. played back home.

"How can you die in a card game?" Pam asked, looking confused as she looked at the cards that I.Q. handed her. "Run out of cards?"

"Crystal traps, troll's breath, dragon flames, there are many ways," I.Q. informed her in a distracted tone, his attention riveted to the big man on stage. You could barely see the tiny scar hidden in his dark colored brow, that he received their first time at Sanctuary by the fairies he kept trying to prove were robots. They all had some Greek ancestry, but I.Q. was the only one you could tell by just looking at his features.

"This game is very popular back home," Telara took pity on her and explained knowing the guys were so caught up in what news Drago was telling them that they weren't going to be very informative. "It's a role-playing game, you can play with cards or play on the game system. Both ways you have your avatar cards with their special abilities and then you have attack and defense cards."

"There is a whole storyline behind it," Chad told her with flair, his eyes bright with excitement.

Pam looked at Telara, who laughed. "The storyline is pretty cool. The Crystal Paladins are from a realm where they are fighting an evil suzerain who rules their realm."

Pam gave her a funny look, "Crystal Paladins? Doesn't that sound familiar to you?"

"Nah," Cole shook his head and Pam gave him a look of astonishment.

"Aren't you the one always looking for similarities between your lives and songs?" Telara had to laugh at Pam's words, sure she was thinking about last year at the concert that led them on an adventure. An adventure that led to them freeing a dragon from his curse, turning him back into the man he was, the same man that soured Cole on thinking there was more to them than just being Guardians.

"Aren't you the one who told me I needed to quit trying to look for things not there?" Cole countered right back, his eyes still on Drago.

"Actually, I think that was your fellow Guardians, not me," Pam told him, her arms folded in front of her as she leveled him with a hard stare.

"This game has been out for years," Chad told her, still watching Drago as he worked the crowd.

Pam looked at Telara, but she shook her head with a rueful grin. "There is no reasoning with these guys, especially when it comes to the Crystal Paladins."

Pam opened her mouth as if to say something, looked at the guys, who were still watching Drago as he spoke of the new expansion set that was coming, and then back to Telara and Tia, who were trying hard not to laugh. "While they love the Crystal Paladins game, they don't think much of the one Paladin we met."

Kull, the fire Paladin who helped Cole realize his potential by putting Tia in danger not even two months ago in Alaska. Who also seemed to look down on them for everything about them, which wasn't fair, but even worse for Cole, who thought they might have had a connection. After all, Cole was the Guardian of fire while Kull seemed to be a Fire Paladin.

"Cole refuses to speak about him," Vanna said, her voice low, although with how loud the room was and how fixated the boys were on the stage, she just needed to be facing away from the boys for them not to hear. "Cole hasn't even gloated about being able to turn his whole body into one big flame and we expected him to be crowing about that for days, if not months." The lights from the room giving her auburn hair a copper glow.

Telara and Tia nodded in agreement. "He actually shut Chad down when he kept going on about it." Tia told Pam whose eyes grew wider. Tia nodded, her blond curls bouncing around her face. While Telara's blond hair was straight, Tia's was wavy, which was a good thing considering her power over the wind. Not as much fixing of the hair when it was already wild and crazy.

"But that was a good thing," Pam said, her voice matching their volume to keep the boys from overhearing although they knew they could hear their thoughts if they wanted. Telara could feel I.Q.'s and Chance's silent agreement. She knew Cole was purposely ignoring them right now.

"It was and is, we're just hoping that when he is able to calm down and forget about what that Paladin did to bring out his powers, he might be more willing to let them out more." Telara spoke, her eyes anywhere but on Cole.

"Wait, he hasn't done anything with his powers since then?" Pam's wide-eyed look would be comical if not for the fact it was serious. The girls shook their heads with a grimace, but before they could say any more, the room erupted in applause as Drago ended his speech with his signature line.

"Don't die!"

ALL TALK ABOUT THE PALADINS AND COLE'S POWERS were forgotten as they enjoyed the fandom all around them, cosplayers dressed up in popular anime, games and other fandoms. A set of boys dressed up like the two crime fighting angel brothers of Telara and Tia's favorite TV series had them squealing with delight when they took pictures with them, which earned them both a weird look from Pam.

They walked by a table where there was a Crystal Paladins card game going on, they stopped to watch from a distance as one of the players crowed loudly as he won again. "Who's the man?" he kept asking in a loud voice, the lights glinting off his glasses even with the ball cap low over his face. He towered over the others at the table except for the guy standing next to him watching with amusement from behind his glasses. They moved away when the ball cap guy started doing a victory dance swinging his arms and crossing his knees.

Pam's eyes grew wide when she found herself alongside a tall, overly thin male who was dressed up as a vampire. An anime character from a series, a vampire cursed in a virtual reality where he is constantly pursued by different supernatural creatures intent on killing him for their mistress. She moved quickly away from him, ignoring the snickers from the guys. Then they came to the booth where the creators of the Crystal Paladins were sitting, autographing different prints of their Paladins.

"We're going to stand in that line?" The freckle-faced, spiked copper-haired Donny stared at the long line waiting for their chance to get an autographed picture of their favorite Paladin, of which you were only allowed one. Donny, who was an Alpha faction member, had come with them along with some other Arions from Sanctuary. Arions were the name given to the residents of Sanctuary, whether they be fighters or otherwise.

The Delta leader Zeke chuckled as he got in line, "You take on shadows but yet cringe at a line? You go check out the marshmallow otters in the next room and I will stand in this big bad line so that I can get my signed copy of Brakus."

"Forget that," Donny blustered and moved to stand in front of Zeke, who, with one turn, had Donny on the floor behind him, glaring up at him.

"No way are you cutting in this line." Zeke smirked down at him, his deep brown eyes dancing with mirth. Zeke was a bronze haired and skin guy who was considered the history buff of Sanctuary.

"Wait, you guys know about the Crystal Paladins?" Cole stood there staring as the other Arions hurried to get into line.

Donny brushed off some stray popcorn kernels that clung to his jeans as he got off the floor. "Why wouldn't we? You act as if we have lived under a rock or something." He gave Cole a disgruntled look.

Cole gave Pam a pointed look, but she didn't look a bit impressed as she responded, "Being an Arion doesn't prohibit juvenile pastimes."

"Hey!"

The protest echoed all around them as the other Arions and all the Guardians gave Pam insulted looks. Pam looked at Telara and Tia, whose voices joined with the others. "You two play this as well?"

"We aren't the best, but we do play on the gaming system. We have our own avatar as well as spell, trap and pet cards," Telara told her.

"Me too," Vanna told them, joining Donny, Zeke and the Theta leader Gabe in line. Her voice held a bit of reprimand, not that Pam noticed, or she didn't care. Unlike the other Guardians, she had never seen Vanna when she went Savage. "Better hurry up, the line is filling up," she spoke, but stared straight ahead as she stood in line and others started filing in behind her. They quickly moved to get in line as well.

"So, which Paladin are you going to get?" Chez, one of the Thetas with red hair and freckles like Donny, asked Chad. Although unlike Donny, while Chez's hair was short, it wasn't spiked.

"The only one worth having." Chad grinned. "Tarmyr."

Chez snorted. "In your dreams, Skeet blows that blowhard out of the water.

"They are just pixels in a child's game," Pam reminded them, but they ignored her as the line moved them closer to the table where Brian sat next to Levi, his bright red fez sitting on his head with snow white puffs of hair peeking out from underneath, signing prints with flair. The two creators of The Crystal Paladins game were chatting up their fans while they signed different prints with smiles covering their faces.

"Cilene could bury them both," Vanna told them, not even looking back as she moved forward.

"And who would you like?" Levi grinned up at Zeke from beneath a bushy, red mop of hair. "Let me guess, Brakus?"

Zeke gave him a funny look and Brian gave a big belly laugh. "Your voices carried; he doesn't have any telepathy powers, no worries."

"Man, you ruined my fun," Levi told him, pulling out a bright blue marker and signing his moniker on the picture of Brakus before handing it to Brian, who did the same.

"We love your game, it's the best around." Cole moved forward, grinning.

"We're your biggest fans!" Chad spoke excitedly as he moved forward.

"Man, you guys have a lot of biggest fans!" Came the very deep baritone voice that could be heard over a room of screaming people.

"Drago!" The boys shouted as their favorite Game Master grinned, coming out from behind the divider behind Brian and Levi.

The big man nodded his bald head at them as he stood there with his arms crossed and his trademark grin that revealed nothing of what was behind those eyes full of amusement. It was the same smile he would wear during tournaments, whether he was winning or not, which would drive his opponents crazy. Usually, they were so nervous they would end up making a fatal mistake. As soon as they heard his iconic *Yooooo-hooooooo*, they knew they were done.

"How is everyone?" Drago nodded at them, winking at Tia,

who blushed and smiled. Cole frowned and the others stared at her; she wasn't one to blush at all.

"We're doing great, we get to meet the genius minds behind Crystal Paladins and the all-time best player all in the same day!" Chad almost plowed over the still glaring Cole to move past Brian and Levi so that he could get closer to Drago.

"You know, Orko, I think we just became yesterday's news," Levi looked over at Brian, whose bushy white hair could be seen peeking around the bottom of his bright red fez.

"I think you're right." Brian looked amused.

"Orko?" Chad looked at Brian, who still wore that contagious grin of his while nodding.

"That would be me!" Brian told them, his arms crossed across his button down shirt that featured multiple superheroes.

"Where did that nickname come from?" Telara asked, as always, the one to speak up where the others faltered. Plus, her curiosity was riding high and she hated beating around the bush.

"From my dear Evil Lyn," Brian told them, which only confused them more.

Levi took pity on them, "Brian shares a mutual love of a cartoon with a fan."

"One of the best ones around," Brian nodded as he signed a print of the female Paladin, Meridot, and handed it to Telara. "You should check it out."

"I'll think about it." Telara nodded as she looked at her print.

"So, what sector do you guys play for?" Drago finally took his eyes off Tia to ask them. In their game there were different sectors that were like guilds. Each sector worked to become the most powerful in the game.

"Minutemen," Chad told him and shrugged. "Not one of the elite sectors, but we do have some good players in there."

"And we're officers," Chance interjected.

"What do you guys think about joining my sector? I can't offer you an officer position, but it is always a possibility if you show you have the right stuff," Drago spoke, looking at them with a grin and something else that Telara couldn't put her finger on. Something that felt familiar.

"You're kidding!" Cole, Chad and Chance spoke in unison as they stared at Drago with the eyes of kids at Christmas.

"If you guys aren't interested," Drago gave a shrug of a shoulder.

"Of course we're interested!" No longer was Cole glaring at Drago, now he was looking like an awed fan.

Drago's laugh boomed out. "Here." He gave them each a card that had a black background with a red dragon outline drawn across the front. "There is my Ipsy site address, go there and sign up with the passcode on the back. I will add you up from there," he told them.

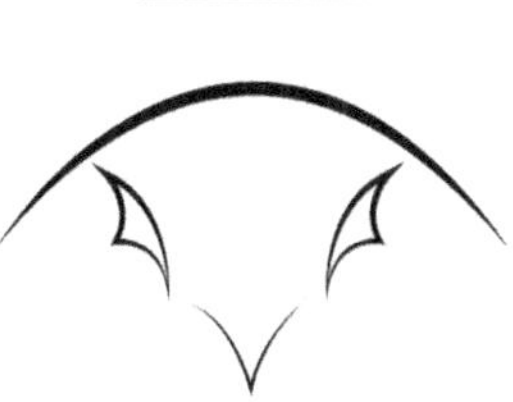

3

THE GUYS WOULDN'T STOP TALKING about being invited to Drago's sector, as they moved from table to table that was still the main focus of the conversation. While Telara was just as excited as the others about joining Drago's sector, it was the elite of the elite after all, but if she had to hear the guys ask which sector they were going to one more time, she was going to drown them in the crystal fountain that sat in the center of the room.

The main attraction at Crystal-Con was the Crystal Paladins game, but there were many attractions from other games and shows. Tables full of jewelry from different fandoms as well as toys of all shapes and sizes. Even clothing like the jackets Cole and Chad were trying on that looked like the tactical ones the agents in the popular T.V. show, *Dawn Riders.*

"Neither of you look like Mart or Jerome," Tia told them as the girls walked by to the next table.

"Mart or Jerome?" Pam questioned.

"The two main actors in *Dawn Riders,*" Telara told her as they maneuvered through the crowd, never realizing how much their obstacle course training would come in hand. "A T.V. show about two agents in an intergalactic agency called Dawn Riders."

"Yeah, the agents actually ride on pure space energy that takes the shape of horses," Chad told her, his voice breathless from him trying to catch up to them, but his eyes held the excitement of getting the jacket that he now wore.

"How much did that cost?" Tia asked him, but when he opened his mouth to reply, she put up her hand. "Never mind, I don't want to know."

"Hey, neighbor." They paused as two cloaked figures clasped their hands to each other's forearms and started talking animatedly.

"Those two characters are from different shows, how can they be neighbors?" Chance frowned at his brother.

"Those two met at a con a few years back, they were dressed up as characters from *Knives Out* who did an impromptu skit that was videoed and went viral." They turned around to see a husky guy standing there, leaning against the wall with a playful smile, his thumbs hooked through the loops on his jeans. His shirt sported the face of the purple paladin, Plax, and on his feet were a pair of worn leather boots, caked mud around the soles.

"They went out for a drink afterwards and that was when they discovered they were neighbors," another voice spoke from the shadows.

"T-man!" Husky turned and grinned at the smaller male who appeared next to him with a lopsided grin.

"Hai." The smaller of the two raised his hand in greeting as he looked at them from beneath his dark brown bangs that fell just over his brown eyes. "Who are the newbies, Re?" He nodded towards the Guardians.

"They are the Guardians." Pam moved to the front of the group and they watched as T-man's lopsided grin grew and his eyes sparkled from beneath the bill of the cap on his head.

"Pammy!"

Pam glared at him. "Trevor, that isn't my name and you know it." She crossed her arms, showing her irritation.

"Awww, Pammy," Trevor said, tilting his head with that grin. "You know you love us."

Pam said nothing but leveled him with one her patented glares so he finally gave a roll of his eyes.

"Fine, Pam." He put an emphasis on her name but her only acknowledgment was a brief nod. Then he turned his attention to the Guardians. "So, these are the Guardians huh?" There was no awe or admiration in his voice, just mild curiosity.

"The ones and only," Cole spoke proudly, holding his head high.

Trevor gave a shrug. "Cool." Then he turned to the one he called Re. "So, have you seen them?"

"Seen them?" Cole asked. "We're right here."

Trevor frowned at him. "I wasn't asking about you, dude, chill." He turned to look at Re, who opened his mouth to respond but a loud, booming voice was heard.

"Aurelius! Trevor!"

They all turned and saw Wes standing there with a big grin, Paul was standing alongside him with the girl they saw after Larry was brought back from his time as a shadow, Jayne. Three of the Arions they had met during their brief stay in Alaska. Wes' eyes got wider when he saw them. "Well, looky here Paul, the Guardians are here as well. We got us a party!"

"Someone who knows how to appreciate us." Cole grinned while Tia and Vanna just rolled their eyes.

Wes looked over at him and snorted. "Knowing who someone is and appreciating them are two completely different things, man. Do we need to pick up a thesaurus?" Wes towered over his girlfriend and Paul, still looking like the quarterback. While Paul was much shorter, they knew that size didn't mean anything when it came to these guys.

"Cole and books don't get along," I.Q. told Wes.

"Not true," Cole protested. "Books can be useful." I.Q. wasn't the only one to give him a disbelieving look. "Target practice, doorstop, fly swatter, the list can be endless." Cole shrugged, ignoring the looks of horror from several of the others around him.

"These are the Guardians that are supposed to be our saviors from the Shadow Master?" Jayne spoke up, looking them over with a glance that showed she wasn't impressed, brushing her long brown from her eyes.

"Hey! Just because Cole is a twit, that doesn't mean the rest of us are," Tia protested and Cole glared at her.

"I'm not a twit!" he glowered at her.

Wes and Paul started laughing. "Man, we have missed having you guys around. Been kind of boring without the comic relief of your standup act, right?" Wes nudged Paul, whose expression denied the words of his best friend. Jayne laughed, moving next to Wes as he wrapped his arm around her shoulders, her head leaning against his torso since she barely reached his shoulders.

"So, who are you guys anyways? You from the Alaskan Sanctuary too?" I.Q. asked Trevor and Aurelius as they walked through Crystal-Con. With their new additions, they looked more like a school field trip rather than a group of friends.

"Us?" Trevor chuckled. "Nope, not even close."

Telara frowned, looking between the two. "Then who are you guys?"

"I'm Trevor and this here is Aurelius." Trevor spoke as Aurelius pulled out a stick of jerky and took off a bite.

"That's helpful," Telara grumbled at them as they stopped at an exhibit showcasing one of the new anime shows about multicolored otters from another planet that teach children moral lessons and general knowledge.

Trevor picked up a pink otter and tossed the guy some bills before pocketing it.

"Pink?" Telara gave him a funny look.

"*Outland Otter*?" Chance had the same funny look on his face.

Trevor shrugged, "My girl loves pink and otters. What can I say? I'm a softie."

Aurelius chortled, "That and you're still in the dog house for going baha-ing on your three-wheeler right through her flower garden."

"Man, you tore up your girl's flower garden?" Paul gave him an incredulous look.

"I might have been trying to show off." Trevor shrugged, "I'll get back in her good graces."

"So, is there another Sanctuary here somewhere?" I.Q. asked nonchalantly, as if remarking about the weather as he looked around at all the exhibits while they moved through the Con.

"Sanctuary?" Aurelius laughed. "No, the only Sanctuary around here is the one you guys are from."

"For Guardians they sure are clueless, aren't they?" Trevor looked to Pam, who didn't look amused.

"The other Guardians never left the Sanctuary," Pam reminded him.

"Until the big bad battle." Aurelius spoke around the Tootsie Roll in his mouth.

"You got into Jeff's Tootsie Rolls?" Trevor laughed. "He's going to kill you."

"Only if he finds out," Aurelius swallowed. "You going to tell him?"

The grin that spread across Trevor's face spelled trouble. "Depends on how much money you got."

Aurelius's face fell. "Dude, they have the best food courts here."

Trevor gave a shake of his head. "Nice knowing ya, man."

"Come on dude." Aurelius held out his hands. "Back me up here, that is what mates do."

"Who said we were mates?" Trevor asked him with a slight tilt to his head.

"Man, that is cold," Aurelius told him under his breath.

"And you guys laugh at us?" Cole turned to look at Wes and Paul, who were in deep discussion. "Are you guys even paying attention?"

Paul looked over at him, "Did you say something?" The others laughed but Cole glared at him. "Problem?"

"This is so unfair!" Cole grumbled and Chad frowned.

"You'll get over it," Wes shrugged.

"So, what are you guys doing here?" Telara asked them.

"Enjoying the Con." Wes grinned and Jayne raised a brow at him. "Wha?" He tried to look innocent but they could tell from Jayne's expression that she wasn't buying it.

Jayne turned to them and smiled, taking sympathy on them. "Kayne sent us down to help the Hunters."

"Hunters?" Cole looked at Chad who looked at Tia who looked at Telara, who looked as stunned as the others.

"That would be us!" Aurelius grinned at them as he walked back towards them with a funnel cake in his hand. They looked around not seeing any food vendors around and realized they didn't even see him walk away.

"Do you ever stop eating?" Chance stared at him.

"Nope," Trevor told them.

"Stazi radioed for us to head back," Aurelius told Trevor, then looked over at Wes, Paul and Jayne. "You guys coming?"

"Of course." Wes nodded at him.

"Where're you going?" Telara asked them.

"Better yet, can we go?" Cole asked his eyes full of excitement.

"Don't know man," Trevor told him. "You got clearance to see our base?"

"Clearance?" Tia frowned at his words, looking around. Telara looked over at Pam, but her expression wasn't revealing anything as she watched Trevor, who stood there with that grin.

"We're the Guardians, that should be our clearance," Chad spoke up looking bewildered.

Trevor snorted. "Here you're just another face in the crowd."

Before they could comment, Paul spoke up, "I don't know Trev, they give some decent comic relief."

Cole, Chad and even Chance gave Paul insulted looks, but Paul was looking at Trevor and ignoring them. Trevor gave a shrug. "Well, if you put that way..." He looked at them. "You're in."

"Seriously?" Vanna looked bemused. "That is all it took?"

"Eh." Trevor lifted his shoulders in a nonchalant manner. "We can always use some comic relief."

"Like you guys don't have enough?" Pam questioned him.

"Nope!" One simple word spoken with a dimple on Trevor's cheek spoke of how much he enjoyed the banter.

"So, where're we going?" Telara asked them as they started walking towards the exit.

"Back to our base," Aurelius told them. "Rogue Hunter Headquarters." He tapped the drawing on his hat. A dome with two slanted lines coming down, two triangles peeking from the slants and a splayed V in the center, below the lines.

"Is that a hawk?" Vanna craned to look at it.

"Do you know of any better hunter?" Wes was the one who asked, and they had to admit he was right.

"Wolves?" Chad grinned while the others rolled their eyes.

"Haven't you ever heard of a hypothetical question?" I.Q. shook his head as they walked out the door into the sunlight.

Trevor and Aurelius made a sharp turn walking briskly down a nearby alley, they had to jog to keep up. "So, what do hunters do?" Telara asked as they moved down another alley and watched as Aurelius pushed a brick in a nearby building. They watched as the cement slab at the base of the building moved and opened up. Wes, Paul, Jayne and the other Arions including Pam jumped down.

They weren't so sure until Trevor spoke up. "What's the matter? Scared?" he asked before jumping down. "Better hurry if you are coming," he called back up. "The hatch closes back up in thirty seconds."

One quick look at each other and around them at the empty alley convinced them they didn't want to be left behind. They took a deep breath and jumped down into the ground just as the cement slab above them closed with a loud thud.

4

"Do you know where we are going?" Tia asked Pam as they walked down corridors underground that seemed to be going nowhere. The walls all around them were cement and cool to the touch. Pipes ran along the walls, Chance mentally told them he could feel the water within while Tia could feel the steam in others.

"To our headquarters." Trevor winked at her as he turned right walking down another cement corridor.

Tia gave him a baleful look, "And just where is your head-quarters?"

"Where we are going?" Telara looked over at Aurelius and saw his lips twitch in amusement, she fought the urge to use her power to trip him, barely.

Pam must have noticed the irritation in the Guardians, "You guys do realize you're irritating seven teenagers with powers, right?"

"Of course they do," Wes chuckled.

Trevor and Aurelius just grinned as they took another turn, this one left and started down a flight of stairs. "These tunnels stretch out under the city," Trevor told them. "We use them when we need to disappear quickly or appear just as quickly."

"You don't have a transporter?" Vanna asked him curiously.

"Sure we do," Aurelius told her. "But when we get a Rogue call and we happen to be in the middle of the city with no transporter around, these tunnels help us get from one place to another quickly."

"This doesn't feel too quick," I.Q. spoke as they reached the bottom of the stairs and walked down another hallway until they came to a dead end, a small balcony with a brown steel railing surrounding it.

"Just wait," Aurelius grinned as he gripped the top railing and vaulted over, Trevor following suit.

"Wha-?" They rushed forward leaning over the railing to look down at the two guys grinning up at them from an over-sized luxury looking mining cart with plush benches for seats. The seat in front looked like a jacked up high back chair with black leather, silver chains and painted flames. Metal levers rose up in front of the chair as well as a metal type of steering wheel, Cole pointed out the silver metal skull on one of the levers.

"You guys coming or what?" Aurelius held out his hands with a goofy grin.

Pam was the next to leap over with the others following one by one. Donny followed his leader with a thud as well as Zeke and Chez. Gabe smiled at Vanna holding out his hand but she just smiled and gave a shake of her head.

"I can handle this," She told him as she ran and vaulted over the railing without even touching it to land on her feet in the cart below and sitting down on the bench, her hands placed regally on her crossed leg smiling serenely up at them.

"Vanna used to be in gymnastics," Tia smiled as she leapt over the railing, a gust of wind could be felt as she all but flew over the railing landing down like a feather followed by Gabe.

Chance took off at a run and vaulted over perfectly landing down with a smirk.

"Dragoon's leading track star as well as swim coach!" Chance held his hands up in triumph. His brother rolled his eyes as he jumped over the railing, not as graceful as Vanna, Tia nor Chance but he landed crouched down on the cart.

I.Q. looked down with an uncertain look as Cole climbed the railing and jumped down landing with a thud. Telara grabbed I.Q.'s hand as they both climbed over the railing so they stood on the other side. They looked at one another. "On the count of three." I.Q. nodded at Telara's words. "One … Two … Three!" Together they leapt down landing on their feet, if not for Pam and Chad they would have tumbled to the floor as Pam steadied Telara while Chad helped I.Q. so he didn't take a nosedive.

"Okay, buckle up boys and girls, destination Citadel," Trevor told them, placing a pair of sports goggles over his eyes sitting in the black leather seat at the front. He grasped the skull lever situated next to his seat, with one movement he pulled the lever back and the cart started moving. Everyone sat down quickly fastening the seat belts around them.

"Citadel?" Telara looked at Pam.

"Rogue Hunters Headquarters," Pam told her as they moved along the rails through an underground cavern that opened up all around them. The weathered stone of the walls around them seemed to emit a chill they hadn't felt until the railing dipped down, making them feel as if they were on a roller coaster.

"Rogue Hunters?" Cole's eyes widened looking at her. "Is that as cool as it sounds?"

"Cooler," Aurelius grinned at them from his seat next to Trevor.

"So, what does a rogue hunter do?" Chad turned back from admiring the stalactites that hung down from the ceiling of the cavern to question.

"We hunt rogues," Trevor hollered back over the noise of the cart's motor moving the wheels along the railing.

"They hunt down rogue Arions and take care of stray shadows that appear," Pam told them, not even acknowledging Trevor.

"Rogue Arions?" Vanna queried. "You mean there are Arions who go rogue? How is that possible?"

"Even though us Arions have Godly ancestors somewhere far down our line, we are still mostly human with human faults." Wes had to raise his voice slightly as they motored past a waterfall that pooled down below in enormous stone like basins.

"I would think the Gods and Goddesses have more faults than humans," Vanna spoke up. "Their powers give them terrible egos and egos tend to ruin everything."

Pam inclined her head just a bit, "She has you there, but Wes is right, Arions are basically humans ... with a kick. Some go rogue because they hate being in the shadows and not getting credit for all the good we do."

"Egos," Vanna interjected.

Pam gave a shrug, "That may be but any Arion who goes AWOL is a threat to what the Sanctuary is trying to accomplish so they must be stopped at all costs."

"Which is where we come in." Aurelius held his head proudly.

"I thought that is what you guys do?" I.Q. looked at Zeke who was in conversation with Gabe.

Zeke stopped talking and looked up at him, "We track them down and monitor them as well as the shadows, some we take care of, but there are times we send the information to the Rogue Hunters and they handle it."

"So, what? Is this like an offshoot of Sanctuary?" I.Q. asked, "Or another whole Sanctuary like the Alaskan one?"

"There is no Sanctuary like ours!" Wes told him while Paul and Jayne both nodded in agreement.

"You know what he means," Chad told them with a frown.

"You'll see when you get there," Pam told them still with the smile on her face.

"And we're almost home," Trevor told them as the cart started to make a climb up on the rails which caused a few of them to grip their seats so tightly their knuckles were white.

"Ummmm, we're going right through the top of this cavern," The panic in Cole's voice was echoed in the gasps of the other Guardians, although when the rocky ceiling slid apart, they were too busy guarding their eyes from the bright sun to freak out.

"Where are we now?" Looking around Telara saw they were in a field next to a country road somewhere.

"Can they see us?" Vanna asked pointing to the car driving along the road not even 15 feet from them.

"Nah," Paul spoke without even glancing their way, his tone calm as if discussing the growth rate of the common grass shard. "Normies can't see past their limited range."

"Limited range?" I.Q. turned to him.

"Normies are mostly closed minded," He shrugged unapologetically.

"Do you have to call them normies?" Vanna glared at Paul but he wasn't paying her any mind.

"Ummm … guys?" Cole's startled voice had them turning to look towards the front of the cart where he was pointing. They felt their stomachs drop when they realized the tracks stop in the middle of the field.

They looked over at Pam, Wes and the others who were talking calmly.

"Hey!" Telara shouted at them, finally they quietened down and looked over at her.

"What?" Wes asked her, looking confused.

Telara pointed at Trevor, "If he doesn't slow down, we're going to crash!"

"Crash?" Paul looked down the railway then back to them as if the railway wasn't about to end sending them crashing into the trees that lined the edge of the field.

"You need to stop and now!" Vanna screamed, but the Arions were looking at them as if they all lost their minds.

"We aren't going to crash," Pam tried to tell them but as they got closer to the end of the railway they weren't listening. Instead, they all ducked down, their arms over their heads protectively as they waited for the crash. The fact they were Guardians with powers not registering in their freaked-out minds, the only thing they understood was they were about to crash and everyone else was acting as if they were still on a Sunday drive.

"You guys okay now?"

They looked up to see Pam smiling down at them and then around them as they realized they were once again under the ground, this time not only were they in an immense cavern but there were buildings all around. The buildings were built into the stone walls and columns inside the cavern, there were stone and metal walkways connecting buildings, some were covered in what looked like glass but they had a feeling they were actually crystals.

"This looks like more than just a military base, it looks like a city." Tia had to grab Cole before he fell over the edge of the cart trying to get a closer look at the buildings all around them.

"Why did you take off your seatbelt?" She glared at him as she pulled him back inside.

"Can't you see this?" He looked at her with wide eyes.

"No," She told him sarcastically. "I have gone temporarily blind thanks to your shining personality."

Cole, who had been about to turn back around to continue

looking at the buildings in the walls and columns, stopped and turned to look at her with a smile, "Really?"

The looks around them went from incredulous to disbelieving. "Don't you know what sarcasm is, man?" Wes laughed while Cole gave a disgruntled look.

"I think that was more hopeful than misunderstanding," Tia tried to hide her smile.

"Have you ever seen anything like this?" Cole went back to looking around them, his irritation with them evaporated as the wonder around them once again grabbed his attention.

It seemed the Guardians were the only ones in awe as the rest just smiled. "This is only one of the many wonders hidden from the world of mortals," Pam told them.

I.Q. looked at her. "There are more places like this?"

"We probably shouldn't be shocked," Chance said. "After all, it was only a few short months ago we were in Alaska listening to a mysterious fiddle player who blows out silver bubbles with videos playing in them."

"Hey," Wes frowned at them.

"There is no place like our Sanctuary," Paul said as he leaned forward, his elbows on his knees while Jayne watched the exchange from her position by Wes.

"So, when do we get to explore this new wonder?" Vanna looked around them with just as much curiosity in her eyes. The cart was moving along the railway under several of the walkways and weaving around many of the stone buildings. They could see some faces in the windows looking out at them, their destination seemed to be the biggest building column in the center of the cavern.

The cart pulled up to a stone landing where the mining cart docked and the two hunters jumped off onto the platform that led into the building. The biggest one, Aurelius turned to them. "First, check in then we can see about getting you a tour."

"Just make sure to fill out the paperwork unless you want to spend several hours trying to get out of the endless maze," Trevor told them as he placed his hand on the wall. The area around his hand emitted a low glow and a doorway opened up in the stone wall right in front of him.

"Endless maze?" Chance looked around nervously.

"Let's just say when it comes to paperwork being done incorrectly, we have a Minotaur that will throw people down the hole into the endless maze and leave them here," Trevor told them as he moved through the doorway.

"She isn't that bad," Aurelius tried to assure them before following Trevor.

Pam rolled her eyes before looking at them, "The guys here, like most anywhere, tend to exaggerate."

"Hey!" Donny frowned at his leader who ignored him as she started after Trevor and Aurelius.

"Let's go, I promise you, Lucy won't imprison you," Pam told them and after a brief hesitation they followed.

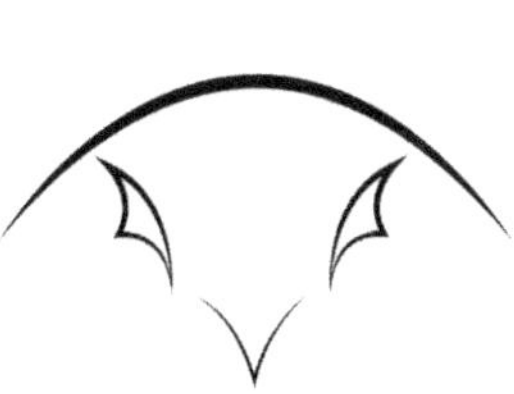

5

THEY WERE FOLLOWING Trevor and Aurelius staring around them as they walked. They had been in Sanctuary with mermaids, gnomes and fairies, who would put spiders in people's beds. They went to Alaska where they met a mystical fiddler and met a nymph who wore all types of mammals as a coat that she threw at a gnome who dared to hunt on her land. You would think they had seen everything, that there was nothing that could surprise them anymore.

As they walked down the stone hallways looking into rooms where there were no doors just openings in the stone walls with no glass where they could see people either training or doing office work, their minds wandering thinking about this new world they stumbled upon.

"Do you see any crystals anywhere?" Vanna whispered to them, looking around they all gave a shake of their heads. No crystals here used to open doorways, lighting up rooms or powering computers.

"We have crystals, they just aren't as prominent as in the Sanctuaries." They jerked around seeing Aurelius grinning, they hadn't realized they were speaking out loud, nor that anyone was listening to them.

"Stazi said they were too ostentatious," Trevor nodded as once again he placed his palm on the wall which glowed before an opening appeared before them.

"Oh, but do you?" They heard a voice that carried even though the person wasn't speaking loudly.

That person might not be speaking loudly, but the person's voice who replied was raised in agitation. "Yes, Jeff, I do! And you are annoying!"

"Oh, but am I?" the person replied and if not for Aurelius jumping back, he might have been run over by the person stalking from a room on the right.

"Just get me the stupid paperwork Jeff." The girl stalked by them, not even glancing their way. "Or you can stay over doing the reports."

"You really want Jeff doing your paperwork, Lucy?" Trevor asked and they watched as the girl stopped then hung her head down with a groan.

"Just get me your paperwork so I can get the reports submitted and filed," she grumbled, going back to stalking into a room where the wall closed behind her.

"Maybe it wouldn't be such a good idea to tell her we need the paperwork for new arrivals." Aurelius looked over at Trevor, who was digging through a big bowl of candy they didn't see on the counter next to them.

"New arrivals?" They turned to see a guy standing next to the opening of the room that they saw Lucy stalking from. They looked from Trevor to Aurelius to the guy they assumed was Jeff. Trevor was the smallest of the bunch while Aurelius was taller but Jeff was taller than both of them.

"Small … Medium … Large." Cole pointed from Trevor to Aurelius to Jeff and chuckled. "Like coat sizes." He and Chad started laughing at his joke. It took them a few moments before they realized they were the only ones laughing. The rest of the Guardians were staring at them along with the Arions, although Telara thought she saw Wes and Paul trying to hold back smirks.

"I like this guy, he's funny," Jeff said before he noticed Wes and Paul standing there. "Wes! Creeper! Hey guys, you ready for some rogue hunting?"

"That's what we're here for." Paul grinned.

"Creeper?" Vanna looked over at Paul, who stood there grinning.

"You don't want to know," Jayne told her as she leaned up to kiss her tall boyfriend, Wes, who leaned down to embrace her. "You guys try to behave while I go visit with Lucy," she told both Wes and Paul before walking past them all.

"Hey, tell her she has new arrival paperwork that needs to be done," Trevor hollered after her, but she never acknowledged him as she moved through the opening into the same room, they knew Lucy disappeared into. He looked back at Wes. "She isn't going to, is she?"

"What do you think?" Wes smirked and Trevor sighed.

"Looks like you get to brave the paperwork dictator's ire," Jeff grinned down at him.

"I think that is above my pay grade," Trevor told him.

"Mine too," Jeff agreed while both Trevor and Aurelius snorted at him.

"So, is anyone going to introduce us?" Telara asked.

"Oh, yeah, guess I can," Trevor said. "Jeff, meet the Guardians. Guardians, meet Jeff."

Telara shook her head at him, "Don't over exert yourself on our behalf," she told him mockingly but he just grinned at her.

"No worries, I won't," he told her his expression one of pure amusement.

She moved past him and held out her hand to Jeff who took it and gave it a shake. "My name is Telara."

"Hello, Telara." He nodded at her.

"Tia." Tia raised her hand.

"Vanna." Vanna gave him a smile and he nodded to her.

"I.Q.," I.Q. spoke up.

"I.Q.?" Jeff asked and I.Q. nodded but refused to explain. "Oh, Lucy is going to have a field day with this, I want to be there when you refuse to tell her what that stands for." He said on a guffaw laugh.

"Self-explanatory." I.Q. shrugged.

"Chad," Chad spoke up from his position leaning against the wall.

"Chance," his brother said, and Jeff looked between the two for a brief moment before nodding in acknowledgment.

"And I am Cole," Cole spoke up, holding out his hand which Jeff grabbed and nodded. "How old are you, man?" he asked, ignoring the incredulous looks from the other Guardians. Jeff gave him a funny look. "I mean, any Arion I have met is young, but you're bald!"

Why Telara was even shocked that Cole would come out and ask that she had no idea. If it wasn't Cole blurting out the first thing he was thinking without putting any thought into it, it was Chad. Yes, Jeff was bald but he didn't look old, at least not in Telara's eyes. She was so shocked that she didn't grab Tia in time.

"Ouch! Woman, what is your malfunction?" Cole shouted, blocking Tia from hitting him again. "I just asked a question."

"A very insensitive one!" she told him, hitting him again.

Jeff disappeared into the room and everyone gave a silent groan.

Way to go Cole, we are going to be kicked out before we can explore this cool place, Chad grumbled via their link while the others gave mental agreements. They had been hoping to check out the other buildings and had been excited to be able to journey across the walkways between them.

Jeff appeared and in his hand was a metal baseball bat that he was handing to Tia. "If you really want to get his attention, then you need Willy," he told her.

"Willy?" She gave him a confused look; this was the first time anyone had ever given her a weapon to use against Cole.

"That is what we call it." Jeff grinned.

"Man, are you crazy?" Cole stared at Jeff with wide eyes and an open-mouthed expression. "You want me to end up in the ER?"

Jeff shrugged, "We have a top-notch Med Unit, they'll make sure you don't suffer too much."

Cole's complete shocked expression might have been hilarious if Telara wasn't so focused on making sure Tia didn't take the invitation. She knew Tia would never seriously hurt Cole, but sometimes Tia's temper was known to get the better of her.

Tia looked at Willy then back at Jeff. "Thanks for the offer but I don't want him hospitalized."

"You never know, it might knock some sense into him," Aurelius said with a grin, ignoring the glare Cole sent his way.

"Don't think that is possible." Chance chuckled.

Jeff shrugged and flipped Willy in his hand before tossing him back into the room where they heard a clang then some dings and dangs as the bat clattered across the floor. "Have you introduced them to Stazi?"

"Nope, figured that was her second-in-command's duty, not a warehouse grunt." Trevor shrugged.

"T-man!" They heard a voice that echoed all around them and sounded vaguely familiar. Turning, they saw the two guys they saw back at the Crystal-Con at the game table entering with a grin. Both wearing ball caps, but their mustaches and stubble showed a reddish orange color.

"Travis! Jessie! How did you guys do?" Aurelius asked.

"The Siamese Battle Twins took the prize!" One of them held up his hands in victory while the other grabbed a water from a cooler on one of the counters that protruded from the walls behind the main counter.

"Hey, Jessie, grab me one man," the one who must be Travis told him. "Be a cool big brother, man."

Jessie walked back with just his in his hand. "Your hand isn't broken."

"It should be after having to carry you through the whole game. I deserve a whole case of water and a cake after all my hard work." Travis told him as he walked over to the cooler and grabbed his own water.

"Your hard work?" Jessie raised his brows at him. "You mean all that hot air from your boasting while I had to back up all your boasts so we didn't lose points."

Travis opened his bottle, taking a long drink. "Not boasting when it's the truth."

Telara looked at the others, wondering exactly what they had gotten themselves into. Her movement caught the attention of Travis who walked over to her and grinned down at her. "Well, hello gurl, how did I miss you standing here looking all fine?"

Telara's eyes widened and she stood there not sure how to answer him, she was sure this was the first time she had someone be this obvious with interest.

"The only thing that could make you look better is being on my arm," He winked down at her and in his eyes, she saw humor, interest and a lot of mischievousness.

"Think she is a bit young for you Trav," Jeff told him and Travis frowned.

"How old are you?" He asked her but it was Jeff who responded to him.

"Have you ever known a Guardian to live past eighteen," he said, then surprisingly looked apologetic before responding, "Sorry, that was a bit cold."

Telara shrugged. "May have been cold but it is the truth."

Jeff gave a solemn nod.

"Still, I'm sorry."

"No worries," she told him with a shrug.

"Will someone answer my original question now?" Cole's voice rose, bringing everyone's attention to him. "How old are you guys?"

"Not as old as you are imagining, but not as young as most you've met." Jeff grinned, doing a fist bump with Travis.

"How is that?" Cole asked him.

"How is what?" Jeff watched him.

"I thought all those in Sanctuary were young like us," Cole said and Telara had to admit she pretty much had the same idea.

Jeff looked at Pam. "How old do they think you are?"

Her eyes narrowed at him. "Watch it, cue ball."

Jeff stared at her for a moment before throwing back his head laughing. "Wow, I think I hit a nerve."

"Man, you have a death wish," Paul told him.

"I thought you guys needed some help," Pam asked, her expression showing her agitation.

"Yeah," Jeff agreed. "Kayne pulled some of our people for a special operation that is going on up there." He looked over at Wes and Paul, who nodded in agreement but gave nothing else away. "So, Stazi had to request some extra help."

"So, who is the rogue?" Gabe asked.

Jeff, Trevor, Aurelius, Jessie and Travis all looked at each other before turning back to face them. Jeff touched one of the three keyboards that were seated within the counter and they heard a melody play that seemed to come from all around them as if in surround sound.

6

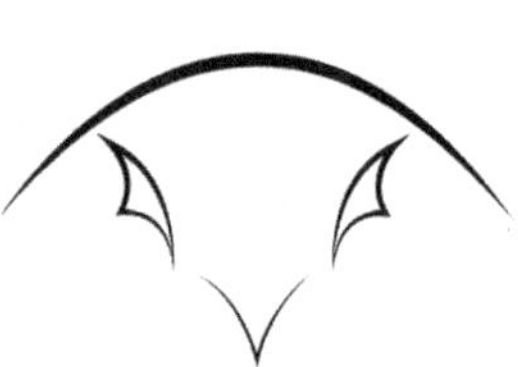

THE SOUND of heels clicking on the stone floor was the only warning that someone was coming.

"Have any of you seen Wes, Paul or Jayne?"

In walked a woman who didn't even reach Jeff's shoulders, her hair falling in ringlets around her face, reaching down to her shoulders. She had a kind smile but her look was that of one in charge.

She could be related to Pam. Chad's mentally spoken words aligned with their thoughts.

Wes and Paul moved forward towards the woman. "Stazi!" Wes grinned clasping her hand in his while Paul gave a small wave in greeting. "Heard you needed the best."

"That is why she has us," Jessie told him as he moved past them into the room where Jeff tossed the bat earlier.

"If that were the case, we wouldn't be here," Paul told him.

"This isn't a time for a size comparison, gentlemen," Stazi's words silenced any more bickering or posturing from the males. She had the attitude and tone of a leader, not someone you would argue with. Then her gaze razed over them and they couldn't stop the butterflies from fluttering. "We have visitors? Have they been cleared?"

"According to them, they are the Guardians and the Guardians don't need any clearance," Aurelius said from around the beef stick he was chewing on.

"Man, do you ever stop eating?" Chance asked, shaking his head.

"No, he doesn't," Travis clapped Aurelius on his shoulder.

"They're the Guardians?" Stazi asked.

"Yes, they are," Pam spoke up. "But I'm sure they'll have no problem filling out any paperwork Lucy wants them to."

Travis groaned. "Give Lucy permission to hand out paperwork? They will be filling in the boxes until they grow old."

"Didn't think Guardians grew old," Telara said then instantly regretted it. The whole mood of the room went from jocular to somber.

"Regardless, we have procedures," Stazi spoke up and Telara was glad someone did. "Follow me and I'll introduce you to Lucy so she can get your paperwork handled before getting you guys situated with your rooms and permissions." She walked past them without waiting to see if they were going to follow.

A quick glance at each other and they moved quickly to follow her through the same doorway Lucy and Jayne disappeared through.

"Is this the biggest room in this building?" Cole asked, looking around him. This room looked to be at least 30 feet wide and just as long or even longer. There were tables with all different types of equipment on them. Some that looked familiar, regular office equipment, and some they weren't very sure of. There were half walls jutting out and several desks as well. In the back of the room was a glass desk with several file holders that were labeled and full of papers.

"Nope, that would be Stazi's." The girl they saw earlier who had stalked from Jeff's office rose from her seat to greet them. "My name is Lucy."

"Lucy, these guys are the Guardians," Stazi told her but there was no surprised look. Stazi looked at Jayne. "You already told her."

Jayne gave an unapologetic shrug. "Had to have an opener."

"I'm really feeling very unappreciated." Cole frowned. "Usually, we get an acknowledgment of some kind."

"Would you like me to jump up and down screaming your names?" Lucy smirked at him.

"Would be a good start." Cole looked back at her, not one hint of repentance in his expression.

"Did anyone ever tell you you're annoying?" Lucy asked him, but it was Vanna who answered.

"All the time."

Lucy looked at her. "And?"

Vanna shrugged. "He takes it as a compliment."

Lucy shook her head. "He must be related to Jeff."

"Hey!" They turned and there was Jeff standing there frowning at her. "There's only one me!"

"Thank the Gods!" That came from Lucy, Stazi, Trevor, Travis and Jessie. Aurelius was too busy eating his Twinkie so he nodded in agreement.

"You could call Lucy the mother hen of the Hunters," Stazi informed them. "She keeps us all in line, makes sure our paperwork is turned in and that we have everything we need for our missions."

"Mother hen?" Cole looked at Lucy then over at Vanna. "No wonder you like her, you two are two sides of the same coin. Both mother hens, just in different ways."

"Yeah, Stazi says that until Lucy tells her to stay away from her 18-9." Jeff grinned, but Lucy shrugged.

"I don't feel like having to deal with the F1s when they are done incorrectly," she spoke while pulling out several pieces of paper and some pens. Handing them to the Guardians, she smiled. "Fill these out and I'll get your rooms ready for you."

"F1s?" Chad frowned looking up from the paperwork in his hands to Lucy, who responded to him as she handed out the paperwork packets to everyone.

"F1s are the error queue from paperwork entered into the 18-9 incorrectly," Lucy told them. "18-9 is where all Hunters enter their reports, some more efficiently than others." She gave a sidelong look at Jeff, who gave a devil may care grin.

Cole looked down at the paperwork in his hand and frowned. "My name, birth date and that I get, but why do you need to know my greatest fear and most embarrassing moment?" He looked up at her.

Lucy looked at him. "Jeff needs to know what types of fears before he can assign anyone for missions; you don't want to have an intense fear of snakes and walk through a reptile exhibit after a rogue do you?"

Tia's face went white as she hurriedly started filling out the forms.

"And plus, it helps when arrogant males irritate me too much, to remind them that I have the key to their deepest, darkest secret." The smile on her face had Cole's eyes going wide as he looked over at Stazi, who looked as if she was barely paying them any mind while she and Jeff seemed to be in deep discussion. Cole looked back at Lucy, who grabbed a bag and slung it over her shoulder. "Finish with the paperwork while I go get your rooms ready, you'll be in the same tower as the Arions."

They expected her to walk past them but instead she hopped out the opening in the back of the room where they could see the outside of the cavern. They ran to the opening and looked down. Lucy glided along on a crystal plate along the side of the building and landed on one of the many walkways.

They watched as she glided in between people walking into a nearby building.

"You guys should get your paperwork filled out and put in her tray before she gets back." Stazi pointed to one of the many trays on Lucy's desk. "You don't want to have to explain to her why you don't have it done."

"THREE ... HOURS ... LATER..." CHAD SPOKE SLOWLY emphasizing each word as they turned in the paperwork and headed out of Lucy's office to where Pam was talking with a silver haired male who stood at least a foot or more over Pam, who wasn't a short person herself. He had a kind smile as he looked over and greeted them.

"Well, if it isn't the Guardians. I am honored to meet you," he said, still smiling.

"Now that is the kind of greeting we're used to," Cole said, smiling at the man and grasping his hand when it was offered.

"I wouldn't put too much stock in what Mark says." Jeff walked around the corner with a clipboard and pen in hand. "He can still remember the big bang."

"Why you..." Mark turned around, raising his fists as if to fight him. "I'll show you old, with one fist behind my back." He put a hand behind his back as Jeff laughed, ducking into his office.

"I don't want to be the reason you need to park in the handicap parking spot," he quipped.

Pam laughed at them both as Mark turned back around and winked at them while Pam took care of the introductions. "Guardians meet Mark, Mark this is Telara, Chad, Chance, Tia, Cole, I.Q. and Vanna."

"Very nice to meet you," Mark smiled at them.

"What is the big bang?" Cole asked, looking confused.

"*The* big bang," Paul told them, entering from the same direction as Jeff had come from. "Don't tell me you guys don't know what that is."

"Sure we do," Cole said, but his expression told a whole different story.

Paul shook his head. "We are surrounded by children, you probably don't even know what an Atlas is."

"Isn't that the Greek God?" Chad asked.

Paul rubbed a hand over his face.

"Back up, Indiana Jones." Looking past Paul they saw a very slender guy with black hair that kept falling down over his eyes and a chin full of dark, scruffy hair as well, walking into the room. He pulled out his phone. "Here in the 20th century, we use a thing that is called GPS."

The look that Paul gave this guy had them all feeling chills, they had really only ever seen Paul laughing and joking, that look was anything but jocular. "James, I think you need to leave now."

James opened his mouth, and the fact that James towered over Paul didn't seem to intimidate Paul at all as he held up a hand. "Op …" He interrupted him. "Just leave, don't pass go, don't collect 200 dollars."

James looked over at them and shrugged. "Fair enough, I was told to tell the Guardians that Lucy has your rooms ready, she put you on floor Aphrodite."

"Aphrodite?" I.Q. glanced at James with a perplexed look, the same look that they all wore while the Arions and Hunters chuckled.

It was Mark who answered them, "All the floors in the guest tower are named after Greek Deities."

"So, what do you call this building then?" Telara asked them curious if it was named after anything Greek.

"The capitol," Jeff told them as he walked back into the room minus the clipboard and pen.

"Doesn't sound too original," Tia said as he moved past Paul and James to start tapping out on one of the keyboards on the counter.

"This is the center of the Citadel." He shrugged. "So, it is the capitol."

They looked at each other but pressed their lips together to keep from speaking out loud the questions that kept running around their heads.

James looked at Pam, "Anyways, I was just sent to relay the message about you guys being put on the Aphrodite floor."

Telara groaned, "Seriously? Aphrodite?"

Jeff laughed, "Have something against the Goddess of love, do you?"

"Yeah, she is annoying and vain," Telara told him, giving a shake of her head.

"You read too many stories," Jeff told her as he moved to flick some switches in the wall next to him, shutting off lights in the rooms.

"No, I have met her … unfortunately." She looked down as she muttered the last part so she didn't see the stunned looks that she received from everyone but the ones who already knew that she had a face to face with the Goddess of Love last year when they were stranded in the town that was cursed by the Gods.

"You're serious?" Mark asked her his expression going between stunned disbelief and mounting curiosity.

Telara wished she had kept her mouth shut, but it was too late now. "Uhhh, yeah." She gave a shrug. "We live in a world where fairies and mermaids are our next-door neighbors, surely talking to a Goddess isn't that big of a thing." She tried to reason, but from the looks she was still getting from them she was sure they disagreed with her.

"Let's get you guys to your rooms so you can relax before the briefing tomorrow," Pam told them then went on to explain when they looked confused. "That is what Mark and I were discussing. Stazi is having a briefing tomorrow about the rogue threat. Lucy will come get you guys and take you to the conference room."

"Why can't we go with you?" Telara looked at her.

"I need to meet with Stazi before the briefing," Pam told her. "But don't worry, you will find more than enough to keep you occupied on the Aphrodite floor." She laughed. "Come on, let's get going so we can all settle down for the night. I will answer what questions I can on the way and show you as much of the place as I can. Cole was right this is more like its own city down here than a military compound, there's lots to see." Pam laughed as their expressions went from suspicious to curious. "Let's go."

7

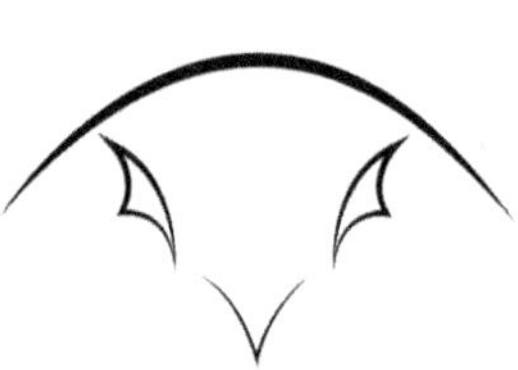

"So, Stazi runs this place?" Telara asked Pam as they walked across one of the stone and glass walkways, several hundred feet above the cavern floor below with the small pools of water, trickles of watery rivers and multicolored rocks.

Pam nodded. "That she does, Jeff is her second-in-command." Pam moved over as a giggling redhead with curls in her hair came skipping by with another girl with blond braids. They watched as the two laughing girls stopped and turned to look out over the banister. As they stood there, another walkway appeared right where they stood and the girls took off running across it.

"Did that just happen?" I.Q. the ever scientific one, the one always looking for a logical answer in the magical world they have been thrown into, asked as he stared at the walkway that disappeared when the girls reached their destination.

"The civilians and others that live here are able to create walkways where they need them," Zeke told them. "Some have some hovercrafts they use but for the younger ones that aren't able to use them yet, they have to use the walkway system."

"Hovercrafts?" Chad and Cole both looked around, their eyes wide with interest.

"You'll see," Donny grinned, his freckled face showing his own excitement. They started moving forward to the column at the end of the walkway they were on.

"So does this place have a name?" I.Q. asked as he looked around them at the columns of stone coming down from the ceiling of the cavern all the way to the floor below. Buildings built within the columns as if they had always been there. It looked like a magical world all around them.

"It is called Rogue Citadel," Pam told them.

"Or R.C. for short," Gabe interjected.

"And some just call it Citadel," Donny laughed.

"Why is this the first time we are hearing about this place?" Telara asked her. "The beginning of summer we learn about a whole new Sanctuary in Alaska and they tell us there are Sanctuaries in more places, now we learn about a whole completely different division of Rogue Hunters?" The other Guardians nodded in agreement with her. "How much more is there that we don't know?"

Pam stopped and looked right at her. "A lot." She told her simply. "I grew up in Sanctuary and there was still a lot that I hadn't learned until I became an actual enforcer at Sanctuary."

"But we are the Guardians, shouldn't we know these things?" Telara asked her; she hated throwing around the Guardian card out there as she didn't want it to look like she was asking for favoritism, but it felt as if this was something they should know.

"Not only are you the first Guardians to see any Sanctuary outside of the one they grew up in, or in your case the Sanctuary you were brought to, but you are also the only Guardians that have ever seen any of the different divisions to Sanctuary and yes there are more." Pam's voice seemed to tighten. "And my only goal is also to make sure that you are the last

Guardians to perish when they face the Shadow Master and his Magine. I'm not the only one, everyone at Sanctuary has been working hard to discover the prophecy that started all this and if there was one that could end it, even Claw has been utilizing any contact he can to dig up anything."

No one said anything as Pam stared at them, not angry but they could feel the emotion in her words and it made them realize how unfair Telara's words were, her words that they all echoed internally.

"I'm sorry," Telara told her and she meant it. The subject of what was meant to happen when they faced the Shadow Master and his Magine was always in the back of their minds but they rarely spoke of it while they learned how to use their powers and Crims to get ready for the battle. They somehow seemed to forget that Pam and their other friends were right there with them.

"We all are," Cole spoke up. "Sometimes we forget we aren't in this alone, but we will try to remember it."

"Make sure you do," Pam told them. "Now, ready to finish the tour and head to your room for the night?"

They all nodded, no one ready to trust their words. They all made silent promises to each other to try and remember to be careful with their words, their friends were trying to help them and they didn't want to seem ungrateful.

Thankfully Pam nodded as if satisfied and started walking again talking about Rogue Citadel and the people who live here. "The building we just came from is called the Capital," Pam pointed to the building they had just left. Telara refrained from saying that Jeff already told them that and let Pam continue. "It is the center of the Citadel and where all operations of the Rogue Hunters are discussed and decided upon. Above the offices, conference rooms and other parts of the headquarters itself are the living quarters where Stazi, Lucy and Jeff live with their families."

"Families?" Cole looked at her. "Again, how old are these people?"

"What is with you and age?" Zeke asked him.

"You do realize how rude that is, right?" Gabe spoke up, a grin peeking out from the sides of his mouth. Cole just frowned at the both of them.

"Where you saw the girls running off to are the living quarters for civilians that either work in administration or some other job other than Rogue Hunting with their families."

Looking over that way, they could see a column that looked larger than the others but more off to the side rather than in the center like the Capital. There were buildings of all shapes and sizes built within the stone, some looked as they could possibly be houses while others resembled apartments of sorts. There were even some stairways that winded around a building out to what could be called a courtyard at the base where a kid was chasing a brightly colored red ball.

Pam pointed to another column just past the one where the kids were running to, where the buildings looked more uniform, square edges all at tight 90 degrees on the buildings with lit up windows. A large entryway opened up to the walkway where they saw people walking to and from, some even in long white coats. "That is the health and wellness column, the hospital is there along with gyms and pharmacies of all types." Pam looked back at them. "If an apocalypse happened, they would be able to survive down here without ever having to go to the surface."

"But then they would miss seeing our handsome faces," Chez quipped but Pam shook her head, ignoring him.

Pam gestured to the stone building they were heading towards, another one built within one of the gigantic columns coming down from the top of the cavern. "This is the guest quarters where every floor is named after a Greek God or Goddess and the amenities there are themed after the deity."

"Yeah, and you had to give us the Aphrodite floor," Telara grumbled.

"That you can blame on Lucy, she chooses where everyone goes but I'll tell you that the Aphrodite floor has the best hot tubs and cafeteria." Pam shrugged. "But, if you really want me to, then I could probably get Lucy to put you on another floor."

"We can suffer the Aphrodite floor," Chance spoke up before any of the others could, Pam and the Arions laughed.

Chad looked around and frowned. "Where did Wes and Paul go?"

"You just realized they didn't come with us?" Vanna asked.

Chad shrugged. "Yeah."

"They stay in Lucy's suite when they come here," Pam told them. "Lucy and Jayne are friends."

"Not to mention Lucy has the hots for Paul." Donny smirked.

"I thought Paul was dating Shayne?" Tia frowned.

"Oh, I'm sure Shayne thinks that way, but never say that to Lucy unless you want her to put you all the way down into the Hades floor, and no one wants that floor," Gabe told them.

"Noted!" Telara nodded and looked around. "So, are these the only buildings down here? You said they could survive down here if there was an apocalypse, where is their food supply coming from?"

"These are the main ones on the walkway system, they also have some down on ground floor with farms, shops and a whole village of sorts that are built within the walls. Some are along the ground floor though," Pam told them.

"Then you have the military barracks that are built into the walls around the cavern but in different areas," Gabe pointed to the wall to their right where they could see some lights on. "That is where the Rogue Hunters sleep and trust me, their facilities put the most luxurious out there to shame."

"Really?" Chance looked over at the barracks.

"Rogue Hunters put their lives on the line every time they go out even more than any Arion in any Sanctuary," Pam told them. "When you're dealing with rogue Arions, you are fighting family and friends, not something that any of us want to deal with."

"Down below you'll see several ornate stone doors that are giant sized." Zeke pointed down and indeed they did see them. "That is where the crystal weapons both offensive and defensive are created, stored and received. They call it the Armory."

"So, this is Citadel huh?" Telara spoke as they reached the doors to the guest quarters.

"All that you will probably see," Pam told them as she placed her hand on the wall where it lit up and the door moved to reveal the opening for them.

"What do you mean that we will probably see?" Telara stopped before she moved past the door.

Pam looked over at her. "Well, we could take a sightseeing trip around Citadel to see all the different parts here, but then you would miss out on the rogue hunt tomorrow and the Crystal-Con. There is so much to this place and for you to even briefly explore the few places you can see with your eyes, it would take up the rest of your summer."

"We can't miss out on the rogue hunt," Chad protested and Telara rolled her eyes and sighed.

"Fine, we won't miss out on the rogue hunt," Telara promised him but silently she felt nervous about this rogue hunt. Most of their fighting had been with Shadows, she didn't know how to handle hunting down an Arion. "Wait a minute," She spoke as she realized something. Pam stopped and turned to look at her. "Are we hunting down a rogue Arion or Shadow?"

Pam took in a deep breath, "That is what we will find out tomorrow, I will be meeting with Stazi in the morning to figure out what would be the best move forward."

"So, Stazi won't tell you?" Telara wasn't sure she liked that idea.

"It isn't that she doesn't want to tell me, just that she needs to get all the details beforehand. When it comes to rogue situations it's best," Pam told her. "Stazi will be having Lucy doing research and intel for the next few hours so that when we do meet tomorrow, she will have all the information. Don't worry, we wouldn't put anyone in the field that we didn't think could handle it." When Telara opened her mouth to protest that wasn't what she meant Pam just shook her head. "Come on, you guys can check out your rooms, grab some food and chill for the night. We will get all our answers tomorrow."

8

———

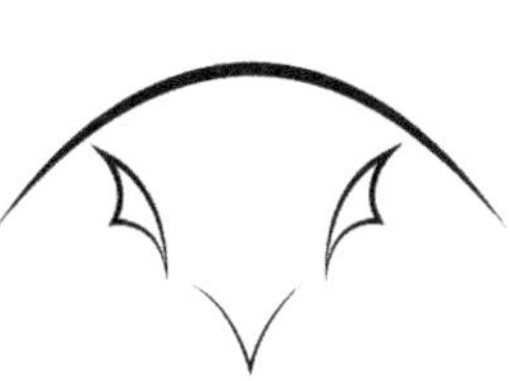

PAM WASN'T KIDDING about the cafeteria, there was a selection that any five-star restaurant would be jealous of. Seafood, poultry, Italian, Mexican, you name it and it was there. The chairs were plush and so comfortable they almost fell asleep in them after eating. Lucy showed up to show them to their assigned rooms, set it up so they could enter with their own hand print and told them she would see them in the morning, after breakfast when she would come to take them to the briefing.

They explored the level and when they got to the Olympic sized pool Chad's eyes almost bulged from their sockets. They had to practically drag him out, reminding him that they needed to get up early for briefing and if he started swimming, he wouldn't get out for hours. The hot tubs were just as enticing and the gym was better than any professional one they had ever seen.

"Man, can we move in here?" Chad asked as they started what felt like a long walk back to their rooms. They all gave a wistful nod; this place was like a dream come true. Alaska was unique but this place gave a new definition to 'luxurious.' "This sure beats our hotel."

They all stopped at his words and looked at each other. Their hotel. "Did anyone think to cancel our reservations and grab our bags?" Vanna looked from one to the other but they all wore the same dismayed look.

Telara gave a groan. "No but it really is too late to worry about it now."

"I can't sleep in my clothes." Tia's nose wrinkled in distaste at the thought.

"Tonight you are," Chad told her and headed to his room, his head already dropping.

"We will get our bags tomorrow," Telara promised Tia, then grimaced as Tia looked so dejected walking towards her room, dragging her feet and she put her hand on the wall. With a sigh Telara followed suit and entered her room.

As soon as her feet hit the soft carpet the lights turned on, not too bright but at a perfect level. She gave a slow shake of her head; this place may not be heaven but it was awful close. No wonder it had the names of the deities, she wondered if this was what it was like living on Mount Olympus.

Telara! she heard Tia squeal via the link they all shared just as she saw her luggage sitting there at the end of the bed.

I have mine as well. They listened as everyone chimed in about their bags being there as well.

Thank the Gods, Cole spoke. *Would hate to have to deal with Tia if she had to sleep in her street clothes.*

Telara wanted to mentally slap him but knew he was correct, even Tia acknowledged it, either that or she was just too tired.

Telara didn't even remember falling asleep, the bed was so soft and as soon as her body hit the mattress she was gone. When she opened her eyes, she felt a familiar presence. She looked over and there stood Zach looking down at her Crystal Paladin signed print she had put on the dresser with a strange look on his face.

She sat up, not ready to get out of the comfy bed yet, and watched him for a few moments before he turned and around and smiled at her.

"Hello sleepyhead."

She pushed strands of hair back behind her ear, tilted her head and smiled back. "Hi there, wondered if I would be seeing you again."

He frowned at her. "What would make you think that?"

She shrugged, "I always wonder that."

"You always think about me?" he asked her and she felt her face grow warm at his words.

"Well, when you want to, you can be very helpful," she told him.

He raised his right brow at her but said nothing as he turned and looked at the print again with that same expression.

"That is a Crystal Paladin," she told him.

"Yeah…" he said slowly as he looked around the room. "This is a bedroom?" She chuckled at his words, the rooms were more opulent and elegant than she was used to, for sure.

"Well, this is the Aphrodite floor." She shrugged and thought she saw his face darken but then he just looked at her and smiled.

"Would explain all the frivolous decorations," he said and she couldn't argue with him. The carpet was so soft you felt like you were walking on clouds and she could say the same of the bed, if she knew what sleeping on a cloud was like. The closet was bigger than her room back home and the bathroom with the garden tub that looked like a small pool would put any royal bathroom to shame, if she had ever seen any.

"So, you just here for a visit?" she asked but sighed at the look in his eyes. "I didn't think so."

"I'm sorry." He truly did look sorry. "I wish it was just for a visit."

She sighed. "Me too, when you come it usually means trouble is coming our way." She cocked her head and looked at him. "I don't suppose this time you will give me straight and informative answers?" She gave him a hopeful look.

"I'm not sure what you mean by straight but my answers have a lot of information in them," he told her and she sighed.

"Didn't think so." She plopped back on the bed debating on whether or not she wanted to hear what he had to say, for a few moments. She knew she would need to hear what he had to say so, after a few more moments she threw the covers back, sliding down to the soft floor where her slippers were. Sliding them on, she grabbed a plush robe that hung on a hook, putting her arms through the arms and hugging it to her body, then she gave a shrug. "Okay, let's go talk in the sitting room."

"Sitting room?" He frowned and she motioned to the French doors. Opening them up, she moved to the chaise lounge and took a seat where she could stretch out her legs.

He moved in and sat down in one of the big lounge chairs where he almost got swallowed up whole. She giggled at the expression on his face. "Is this a chair or quicksand?" She started to laugh harder as he pulled himself out of the chair and sat down on a padded bench. "Much better." He looked at her. "I like it when you smile, you should do that more often."

Even as she smiled at his words, she knew that their time was limited as it always was, since they met when she was first brought to Sanctuary and he helped her to realize their powers in a dream, although she was never certain if it was only a dream, since she saw him before they left the Sanctuary. Pam thought he had been a prophet, which she said was worse than a ghost since they never gave too much information and a lot of questions.

Time to find out what mysteries and half explanations he brought her now. "So, why are you here?" She asked.

He gave a small smile and in that smile, she thought she saw regret but wasn't sure. Whatever it was, it was gone as quickly as it showed. "I am here to warn you not to go on the mission with the others, the danger is too great."

Telara frowned at him. "Too great? Greater than taking on the Shadows?" He had warned her of danger a few other times before, when they went to the island where they discovered a town cursed by the Gods and then he had given some helpful advice during their time in Alaska, but he never told her not to go.

"Taking on the Shadows, you know who is your enemy," he told her. "Battling a rogue Arion isn't as cut and dried."

Telara shrugged. "We'll have Pam and the Hunters guiding us. We will be fine."

He gave her a searching look and sighed, "This rogue they are hunting, I feel he will test you beyond what you are ready for."

"You worried I won't pass?" she asked, not sure if she felt insulted at his words or worried by them.

"I am worried you won't survive." He looked at her and she could see the worry in his eyes.

"What won't I survive?" She asked him. "Fighting an Arion? I have survived fighting the Shadows back at Sanctuary, the Goddesses on Lapros as well as the evolved Shadows in Alaska with the cloaked woman. Why are you worried about a rogue Arion, how can they be more dangerous than the Shadows?"

"Nothing is more dangerous than losing one's self and that is what you are in danger of with this battle," he told her.

"This sounds a lot like what you said before we went to

Lapros." She watched him as she spoke, he nodded but said nothing. "You give me warnings but they are so vague that I don't understand them, by the time I do it is too late. How do you even know these things you tell me? Why can't you tell me everything?"

"I want to tell you more but we can't always do things the way we want," he told her. "I can tell you this rogue will test your faith and that is dangerous for you." He rose from the bench walking towards the window that looked outside into the cavern around them.

"Why me?"

"Trusting isn't your strong point," he told her and while she wanted to argue with him, she knew he was right. "Your trust issues could not only be your downfall but that of those you love."

"So, you tell me who to trust," she told him. "You were a Guardian once, surely you know who I can trust and who I can't?" She asked him.

He turned to frown at her, "Why do you think that?"

"You can tell me how to avoid a death like yours," she told him, feeling a bit callous speaking of his death in such a casual manner but the point was that he was dead and they needed to avoid their deaths. The fact that every Guardian who faced the Shadow Master and his Magine perished was something they couldn't put out of their minds. It was something that many in Sanctuary were trying to figure out how to prevent.

The look in his eye made her regret bringing it but his words puzzled her even more. "I don't know how I died. I don't remember my own death."

"You don't?" So much for that idea, she tried to keep the feeling of self-pity at bay, hoping he didn't sense it. He just shook his head. "Do you even remember going to battle the Magine?" Another shake of his head.

"I'm sorry, I wish we had more time," he told her and she

felt bad for making him feel bad. With a sigh he told her, "It's time for you to wake up."

SHE OPENED HER EYES AND SAW TIA LOOKING DOWN at her. "You going to get up for breakfast before they leave without us?"

Telara looked around her room but there was no evidence from her talk with Zach last, her print still on the dresser, where Zach looked down at it last night. She sighed then shook her head when Tia frowned at her. "Will tell you over breakfast, I'm famished."

9

"So, another warning that doesn't explain what we are being warned about?" Vanna asked as they sat there eating eggs, bacon and hash browns.

Telara nodded, her mouth full of eggs. While Telara didn't want to speak with her mouth full, Cole had no problem as he almost spit his food out when he spoke, "Did he tell you anything about this rogue?"

"Ewwww," Tia complained and with a wave of her hand she sent all the food he spit on the table back at him with a gust of wind.

"Hey!" He protested, "I was just asking a question." He wiped the food from his face.

"Next time make sure you swallow your food first." Tia glared at him.

Telara spoke up before the battle could get any more tense, "Just that the rogue would test my faith."

"Faith in what?" I.Q. asked her, but she shrugged.

"I don't know for sure, but he also spoke about me having trust issues, so that could mean our belief in Lucius and what he has been telling us," she said, starting to play with the food on her plate.

"So, do we go or do we stay?" Chance leaned back in his chair and looked at her.

"I'm going." She shrugged. "Up to you guys what you want to do, you know I won't pressure you to do anything that you don't want to. Not like this would be the first time we discover we had been lied to."

"True dat." Chad grinned stabbing at a piece of sausage before taking a big bite of it.

"So, was this man-made or natural?" Chad asked Lucy as they followed her along the walkway heading towards the Capital where the others waited for them.

"Natural," Lucy told him. "We discovered it and then created what you see here."

"What, did someone fall through a crack in the ground and discover this place?" he asked then looked up. "And did they survive the fall?" A few of them shivered at that thought.

Before Lucy could answer, I.Q. piped up, "Most likely they discovered the cavern by digging where they shouldn't." Lucy turned and looked at him through narrowed eyes but I.Q. didn't bat an eye as he continued, "Most caverns are created from the dissolution of limestone under the surface of bedrock so many don't have an entrance until man creates one."

"Or, one falls in," Lucy told him, her irritation that he took over her duty as tour guide evident in her voice. I.Q. nodded in agreement.

Cole laughed. "Man, since coming to Sanctuary and learning all about magic and fairy tales being true, we kind of forgot that you were the brainy one of the bunch."

Now it was I.Q.'s turn to look irritated as he leveled that

look on Cole. "Would you like to be the one to try to decipher the star gazer?"

Cole held up his hands in surrender. "Not me, I can't figure that thing out even when you try to dumb it down for us."

I.Q. nodded, satisfied as they reached the Capital and followed Lucy inside.

They passed a room where there was a bay window opening and they could see a spacious office there with a nice sized oak desk in the center, the walls were lined with bookshelves that were filled with books and other knick knacks that looked as if they came from all around. They saw Stazi and Pam seated, having what looked like an intense conversation if the looks on their faces were any indication. There on the desk sat a crystal rose that looked so lifelike, they wondered if someone had.'t crystallized a rose, they could feel Vanna's irritation that someone would do that and were quick to mentally remind her that they didn't know for sure, it was only an observation.

Lucy gave them an odd look then glanced into the window where Stazi looked up, noticed them and then the window became a wall they couldn't see in.

"It isn't nice to peek into windows," Lucy told them motioning for them to follow her down a corridor.

"Then maybe they should put some blinds or shades up," Cole countered, ignoring the glare from Lucy as they entered the conference room where Wes and Paul were already seated with the other Arions from their own Sanctuary. Lucy moved away to sit down next to Jayne on the other side of the room and start talking, their voices too low to hear although they were sure they didn't want to know what was being said with the glares that Lucy was sending their way.

"So, the Guardians decided to join us on our hunt." Trevor walked into the room, a coffee travel mug in hand. On the mug was the same symbol that they wore on their hats.

They nodded, but it was Telara who spoke. "Well, we didn't

want you to bumble the whole hunt so we figured we would give you a hand."

Are you trying to get these guys going? Tia spoke via their mind link, staring at her friend as if she had lost her mind. *These guys invented boasting, haven't you been listening?*

Telara grinned at her and nodded, responding back, *Yup, why do you think I did that? These guys either have big egos or are just annoying. Either way, I wanted to give them some of their own medicine.*

Cole looked confused. *I thought that was our job?*

Telara shrugged and the sound of Gabe clearing his throat let them know their mind speaking didn't go unnoticed.

Just in time, Pam and Stazi entered the room with the other Hunters and a few that they hadn't met yet. One who walked in, taking a seat but saying nothing. His expression was of one who had no time for jocularity, he was there to do a job and nothing would get in his way.

"That's Spencer," Trevor told them, but Spencer didn't even acknowledge them as he waited for Stazi to start the conference. "Don't take it personally, he doesn't like anyone."

"Just because I believe we should worry more about getting the job done before goofing off doesn't mean I don't like anyone," Spencer told him, then turned to look at Trevor, his grey eyes hard under his hat. "Just means I am good at what I do."

"Numbers don't mean anything," Trevor scoffed. "It is how the deal is handled that shows the true master."

Spencer turned back to look at Stazi who just looked at all her Hunters with the expression of a proud leader who wanted to let them enjoy a bit of razzing each other before getting back to business. Although, when they looked at Pam, they could see the worry lines around her mouth and eyes, something that made the butterflies in their stomachs start to flutter again. Also made Zach's warnings blare with big red lights in Telara's mind.

"All right, let's get this meeting over with so we can get out there and get the rogue off the street and in custody where he belongs," Stazi spoke up without even looking behind her. "Lucy, hand out the briefing pamphlets."

Jayne started whispering to Wes while Lucy handed out the pamphlets to everyone before moving back to her seat next to Jayne, looking at Stazi as if to say she was ready.

"Kiss up," Chad muttered, then realized exactly how silent it was in the room when everyone looked at him. His face went a dark shade of red as he muttered an apology, although more than a few of the faces around the table were trying to hold back their grins.

The lights went down and in the center of the table a screen showed up and a vision of a young man with dark features appeared. His eyes seemed to be looking at every one of them, his chin darkened with some stubble as well as a few scars that only made him look more dangerous, or, in Telara's opinion, more handsome. The minute she thought that she heard the derision that came from Cole, Chad and even Chance. She grinned but said nothing as she waited to hear about this male she truly hoped wasn't the one they were hunting, but she had a faint feeling he was.

"Many of us at this table know our mark," Stazi spoke up and then looked over at the Guardians. "Except for our new friends." They nodded in acknowledgment and she continued. "Flint, one of our best Hunters. I won't lie to you and tell you this will be easy. Flint won't be easy to take down."

"Heck no he won't, but we won't let that stop us," Travis spoke up and the others nodded.

"Remember, he's still one of our own," Stazi spoke while some of the others nodded. Telara noticed how Pam stared at the image on the table, not even acknowledging the reactions or words from around the table. "We will take him in, but even if he has faltered, he is still a Hunter who deserves to be taken in with respect."

The expressions around the table varied but the one expression was mirrored by all, the look of determination.

"But he still needs to be taken in and not to be underestimated," Stazi continued. "We take him in and we do it with respect but also," Stazi paused and took a deep breath before continuing with a look of regret, "we do what we must to keep the casualties to a minimum."

The heads around the table nodded in agreement, and Stazi spoke again. "Open the pamphlets in front of you, that is the intel we have managed to round up on Flint. He has made some appearances and while his intentions haven't been discovered yet, he has been more active than you would expect from a rogue. Follow the leads and see if you can bring him in before he does something he won't be able to come back from."

Looking down at the pamphlets and turning the pages, they saw photos of the man on the screen conversing with a gnome who had a disgruntled look on his face, his beard unkempt and as unruly as the gnome himself with his tattered clothes and boots where you could see one of his dirty toes sticking out.

"But we do have an ace in the hole," Stazi continued and she looked right at the Guardians, which caused them to look at each other wide eyed and a bit freaked out. "Seven of them."

"How?" I.Q. looked at her, asking the question they all wondered.

"Flint knows how we fight," Stazi told him and then looked at each of them. "He has even fought with the Alaskan Sanctuary and knows some of their fighting techniques, but he has never met you. While he was taught about the Guardians from a young age, he never got to meet you and from what we have been told you seven are nothing like any of the previous Guardians."

"From what we have been told, we will take that as a compliment," Telara told her.

"But how do we fight one of our own?" Cole asked her. "We know how to fight the Shadows but how do we fight one of our own?"

Stazi looked at him with a grin. "I'm glad to hear you say that."

Cole frowned at her. "Say what?"

"The fact that you don't try to elevate yourselves above the rest of us, I have to admit that our first impression made me wonder, with some of the things you said." Cole gave a chagrined look at her words, but she just continued speaking. "I can't tell you what to do, I just know that Flint knows how we fight. What we need is the element of surprise … you." She stood up and looked at them. "Just remember, this isn't a mindless Shadow you are dealing with. Take every precaution and don't drop your guard."

The lights came on in the room and everyone stood up. Stazi spoke as they started to head out of the room, "Follow Lucy to the armory where she will get you suited up with some new toys that will help with the mission. Jeff is running lead."

THEY WERE WAITING OUTSIDE THE ARMORY FOR LUCY, standing next to Jeff as they watched Trevor and Travis moving crates around with hoverlifters. They resembled forklifts except with an Arion makeover. Where the wheels would be normally were the hover disks that enabled them to move over any terrain easily. Their forks looked a bit more advanced, with a flip of a switch the forks could curl up to keep a better grip on the crate. The one thing they couldn't figure out was the bumper pads all around the lifter.

Jessie and Aurelius were inside the armory getting everything rounded up for them while Pam stayed behind with Stazi.

Trevor and Travis had been getting loud with each other as they moved around each other narrowly missing side swiping each other with each turn.

Am I the only one who feels as if I am watching an episode of Cole and Chad?

They couldn't hide their chuckles at Tia's mental question. Jeff gave them a funny look but they refused to even acknowledge it as they watched the show in front of them.

"Quit being a Sally, man!" Trevor snapped at Travis, who was moving a crate on his lifter.

"I'm not a Sally, you are!" Travis spoke loudly as he moved his lifter behind Trevor's.

"No, you're the Sally, Sally!" Trevor called back as he moved to pick up the crate Travis left.

Telara looked over at Tia who was pressing her lips together to stop her laughter and failing miserably. This was better entertainment than watching Cole and Chad fighting over the last piece of pizza.

"Hey!" Both Cole and Chad spoke verbally.

Jeff looked over at them again. "Personal issues?"

"Something like that." Telara grinned, ignoring the glare from Cole and Chad.

"How can I get my work done with you always getting in my way?" Trevor yelled at Travis as he zoomed in front of him.

"Get out of my way!" Travis yelled back at him.

"No, you get out of my way!" Trevor shouted as his lifter rammed into Travis who turned around yelling at him.

"Now we know why there are bumpers," I.Q. spoke watching them.

"Sally!" They weren't sure which one shouted this but it echoed around them.

Tia turned to look at Jeff. "Okay, I have to ask, what is with them calling each other Sally?"

Jeff just shrugged as he watched them.

"That's their own way of insulting each other," Lucy appeared behind them.

Telara looked at her. "By calling each other Sally?"

Lucy jerked her thumb at Jeff. "He started it, ask him."

Jeff gave an uncaring tilt of his head. "No idea what you are talking about."

Lucy rolled her eyes then looked up at Jeff who wasn't even looking at her, but watched Trevor and Travis lift up a crate to where Aurelius appeared in an open doorway in the building several feet up. "Yes, Satan?"

They turned to look at Lucy, expecting her to go off on him, after all he had just insulted her, but she just told him, "Armory room Calypso is stocked with gear and crystals for you guys to gear up."

"Is everything here named after something Greek?" Cole asked.

"When you let Lucy name them it is," Jeff told them, turning away walking towards the armory.

"I maintain it, I name it," Lucy said simply, walking away from them.

They jogged to catch up with Jeff. "So, why Sally?" Telara asked.

Jeff shrugged. "Why not?"

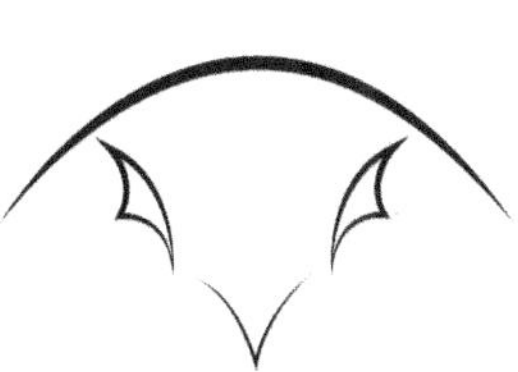

10

———

CHAD AND COLE stared at the Hunters as they pulled on their dark leather jackets with chains with crystals of different types to handle all types of situations they might run into. Illusion crystals that might be needed to keep their actions secret from any civilians they might run into, healing crystals needed in case of any injuries as well as some memory crystals. Not to mention some neat new gadgets.

They looked at Pam, who stood there in jeans and a dark jacket.

"Should we suit up?" Telara asked her and she felt the relief from the others that she asked, mostly from the guys who didn't want to sound silly.

Pam shook her head and gestured to the lockers where dark jackets hung from hooks. "We will be going out among people and trying to blend in so civilian clothing will be best, but those jackets will also offer more protection." She stopped for a moment then looked at them. "Although it wouldn't be a bad idea to keep the suits in the back of your mind in case, good thing Claw came up with the insta-suit feature for our Crims."

"I heard about those." Trevor looked up from attaching his crystal gadgets to his belt. "Not that we were ever interested in them."

"Who needs insta-suits when you have insta-studs?" Travis grinned, pulling on the edges of his leather jacket while Trevor laughed.

"Got that right!"

Vanna looked over at Cole and Chad. "I thought you two held the market on egos, I think these guys are going to give you a run for your money." Several in the room chuckled, but Pam a few of others barely cracked a grin.

Tough room, Cole spoke via their mind link, which was probably a good thing right now.

Don't forget this rogue is a friend of theirs, I.Q. reminded them and they all agreed mentally with him about doing their best to keep their expressions as neutral as they could.

Spencer walked over to them, handing them each a leather pouch, his words not unkind but they also spoke of the seriousness of what they were about to face. "In here you will find crystal bombs, illusion crystals, capture nets and tracker signals. Is there any that you need a tutorial on?"

Cole grabbed his pouch attaching it to his belt with a snap. "We've been through Shadow battles before, I'm sure we can handle it."

Telara snorted at his words. "You may feel confident enough to stumble through trying to use these gadgets in the field, but I would be more confident if I was shown how they worked."

She almost thought she saw Spencer smile but if she did, it was either really quick or real small. He reached into his own pouch and proceeded to explain each item and how to use it. "Each item works with just a thought as you touch each one. The crystal bombs will heat up with the adrenaline from you and explode on contact when you throw them, they will not activate without touching your skin first. Different from many of our old defense artillery where the crystal couldn't touch the skin." This time she was sure she saw a smile there. "Which, I hear, we can thank you and your crystal essence wielding."

Telara gave a shrug and lifted her arm where the Rotary sparkled and shined. "Not me, but my Rotary."

Spencer gave it a curious look before pulling out the next item. "Illusion crystals work with your thoughts and with a Guardian whose power is in the mind, I'm betting you could do more than the brightest healer with this." Telara looked at the crystal, then gasped as it glowed. "Use this when we need to be concealed, placing it in strategic areas can make the people see either an empty field or just give them the sensation of being repelled from the area. Depends on the user."

The next one he pulled out Tia grinned. "Capture nets, we used those on the big battle with the Shadows at Sanctuary."

Spencer nodded. "Pushing a button will release a net that will capture and transport a shadow to a holding cell."

"What about the tracker signals?" Cole asked, his curiosity finally getting the better of him.

"Not so sure of yourself?" Zack chuckled, but Cole ignored him as Spencer pulled out the metal looking poker chips with multicolored crystal lines weaving around the surface.

Spencer showed them the metal button in the center of the chip, "If we get separated and you discover yourself in trouble," he began and pushed the button. As soon as he touched it their belts all lit up and they felt a vibration that seemed to gravitate towards where Spencer stood. "Everyone else will then drop what we are doing and head towards the tracker." With another press of the button, it stopped. "But only the person who activates it can deactivate it."

"Okay, school's over, let's get going," Jeff announced, grabbing a satchel that he slung over his shoulder. "Lucy has the hovercrafts ready for us."

"We get to ride hovercrafts?" This time Cole and Chad's excited faces mirrored the others' as well.

Jeff raised a brow at them. "Just don't wreck them, Stazi will take it out of your hide."

That took some of the excitement out of their expressions, some but not all. They followed the Hunters and the other Arions out of the Armory down a stairway coming out on the floor of the cavern where there were the hovercrafts there in front of them hovering above the ground. Combination between a motorcycle and a four-wheeler, with two large hover disks where the wheels should be.

Spencer and Jeff quickly gave them a quick tutorial on them, more crystal upgrades to help conceal the hovers or turn them into an offensive or defensive vehicle.

"Static!" Cole and Chad both breathed, their eyes showing their admiration.

"Hunters!" Jeff spoke then looked at the rest of them, "And guests." Telara and Tia smiled at him. "Let's ride."

Hunters, Arions and Guardians climbed on the nearest hovercraft to them with grins on their faces as they all gripped the handles revving up their rides. Jeff nodded to Spencer who took the lead moving his hover up a path that led to the back of a cavern and into a tunnel in the wall.

THEY STOOD IN AN EMPTY FIELD WITH NO ROAD OR any sign of civilization for miles around, their hovers quietly running but staying in one place waiting for their riders to come back to them. They had followed several of the leads from the reports and now they found themselves standing there. Chad made squishy noises with each step from his fall into the swamp earlier.

Only hours ago, during their trek into a swamp that was

hidden from outsiders, Jessie tried to warn him to be careful, there were Kelpies in the water and they tended to be playful, some downright mischievous. It didn't help that Trevor and Aurelius egged him on. They were all on the dock outside the hut that was in the middle of the swamp, waiting, while Jeff, Spencer and Travis went inside to speak to the nymph they said lived there.

"Why would a nymph live in a place as creepy as this?" Chad had asked, looking around the swamp at all the overgrown vegetation on the banks and the eerily looking trees that grew from there as well as the swamp itself.

Trevor and Aurelius were grinning at each other, something they knew from experience with Cole and Chad meant trouble, but it seemed Chad wasn't paying any attention to them.

"Could have something to do with the magical properties of the swamp water in this particular area." Aurelius grinned pulling out a piece of jerky and taking a bite.

Trevor bumped into Chad as he passed by him, heading to where Aurelius was standing. "That could be it."

That got Chad's attention and he looked over at the murky looking water but only saw his reflection in the clouded surface. "Magical properties?"

Telara looked around at the others who were either rolling their eyes or shaking their heads, she hoped that Chad wasn't buying into this. Granted, their lives were anything but normal and magical water probably wasn't a far-off possibility, but the grins on the faces of Trevor and Aurelius was a dead giveaway. To some of them.

Chad bent down under the railing and looked closer at the water, just as a Kelpie reared its watery, horse-like head out of the water, grabbing the collar of his jacket and pulling him into the swampy water with a loud splash.

Trevor and Aurelius' laughter echoed off the trees around the swamp as Trevor pulled out a small metal box with a crystal button from his pocket while the others rushed to help Chad out of the water. As they reached the railing, they saw Chad rising out of the water as if by wind. Telara looked at Tia, who shook her head. "Not me, I didn't even think about using the wind to help him out."

"Well, I didn't do it," Telara said then looked back at Trevor, who had the box in his hand and pointed at Chad, who floated over to him before dropping onto the dock.

"No worries man," Trevor told him. "We got your back."

Chad frowned up at him. "After setting me up to take a dive in that muddy pool."

"That's our Trevor," Jeff spoke with a huge grin as he left the hut. "He is the type of friend who will hand you a parachute before pushing you off the cliff." That got some laughter while Trevor gave a proud little grin and shrugged as he pulled out a crystal disk from Chad's pocket.

"Any luck?" Jessie looked at his brother, who shook his head.

"Seems Flint is making sure not to stay in one place too long," Travis told him as he hopped on his hover, then looked back at Chad. "Keep a good distance from the water and the trees, Kelpies aren't the only things that like to cause chaos in this swamp."

"Yeah, the Gremlins like to hide in the trees waiting for their victims." Trevor said hopping on his hover and heading out over the water with a much more cautious Chad.

Now, it was several hours later that they were standing in that empty field, Chad still casting Trevor and Aurelius baleful looks with each squish. "So, what are we doing here?" Chad looked around.

"Waiting," Jeff said, still seated on his hover staring out over the empty field as if he was indeed waiting for something. For what, they didn't know.

"At least you don't have to worry about any water horses

this time." Cole grinned at his friend who glared back. "I told you that I would help dry you out."

"Wasn't taking the chance that you would end up over cooking my clothes," Chad grumbled and Cole shrugged.

Tia shrugged. "I could try to help dry you off." Chad didn't look any more impressed so she pressed her lips together and turned to look out over the empty field as well.

"What are we waiting for?" Telara could no longer hold back the question, she wasn't known for her patience.

"You'll see." Jessie smiled and winked at her.

Cole held out his hand staring at it intently while they watched him, mainly for something to do as they were all getting antsy just standing there. Pam was watching Jeff. She hadn't spoken much since this morning's briefing and while Telara wanted to question her, she had a feeling it was something better left for later.

A sound had her turning to see a flame burning brightly in Cole's hand illuminating the grin on his face while they all looked on.

"Be careful," Vanna told him, watching him closely, ever the watchful mother nature, especially when it came to Cole's flames.

Chance moved by his brother pulling the water from his brother's clothes and putting out the flame in Cole's hand which brought a frown from Cole. "Hey!" he protested, but Chance shrugged.

"Chad needed to dry off and you needed to be watered down before Vanna went Savage on you."

Hard to argue with Chance when Chad was no longer making squishing sounds and Vanna's frown had dissipated. A gasp had them all turning to see where Tia was pointing, where only moments before had been an empty field a magical, rundown little village shimmered into view. At first it was nothing but a blur, but after a few moments they could see grass houses with other buildings that were either built into trees or hills that hadn't been there moments before.

"Welcome to Claramere." Jeff nodded at them hopping down off his hover. "Let's go have a talk with Leroy."

"Leroy?" Tia looked at Telara, who shrugged as they moved to catch up with everyone else.

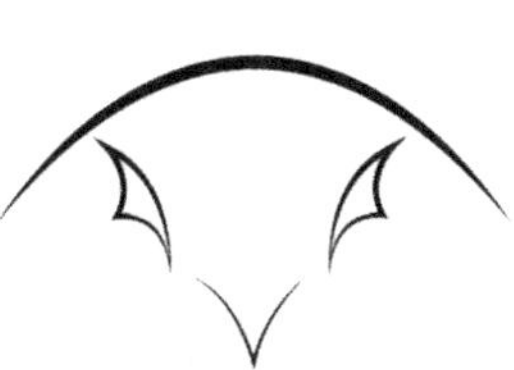

11

THEY WALKED through the village looking around them at the houses where they saw little faces looking out at them from behind the scraps of fabric over the windows or behind the panes of dirty and broken glass. "Is this a town of gnomes?" Cole asked looking around, it wasn't easy to tell when there wasn't anyone about although the fact that the grass and stick houses resembled playhouses they had as children.

"Gnomes are only a few of the residents you will find here," Jessie told them as they passed by a small home where they saw a pair of eyes peeking out at them with a furry face. "Goblins, Gremlins, Trolls and Gargoyles are just some of the residents that also reside in this town." He continued speaking while they walked past a few other homes that vary in sizes.

"Gremlins?" Chad stopped and looked around as if expecting some green little guys to jump out at him.

"No worries," Jeff told him as him and Spencer walked past him. "They don't attack unless you stand around and gawk at them."

Chad jerked around his eyes wide staring at Jeff's back, then he turned to Trevor who was coming up on them. "Is that true?"

Trevor said nothing and kept walking.

"Is it?" Chad looked around but everyone was laughing.

"Let's go, we need to find this Leroy," Telara grabbed his arm and pulled him along, trying not to laugh as he stared straight ahead this time. Jeff and Spencer stopped at the door in a grassy hill that towered over them but yet still looked like it would be too small for them.

Jeff turned to look at them, his expression serious. "All joking aside stay close and don't wander off while in here." He stood there looking at them, when they realized he was waiting for them to acknowledge what he said, they nodded. He nodded back to them and then turned and went through the door.

They weren't sure what to expect when they entered, but what they saw was a tavern like atmosphere with wooden tables and oil lamps keeping the darkness at bay. This place reminded them of Silest's tavern back at Sanctuary, a place out of time but not because of a curse like Lapros. Jessie wasn't kidding, there were gnomes, goblins, trolls along with many other types of mythicals.

In the corner sat a hag staring into her cup but Telara couldn't shake the feeling that something felt familiar about her. She looked at Tia, who was watching the hag as well. Long, silvery, grimy looking hair hung limply down around her face. She wore a cloak that had seen better days, there were tears and dirt as if she had pulled it from the trash. Her nose resembled one you would see on one of the witches' masks they wore at Halloween as children, they weren't for sure but they could almost make out a wart on the end of her nose.

A loud noise pulled their attention from the hag, Spencer stared down at a gnome seated on a stool at the bar and his expression was anything but friendly. The gnome they saw in the reports back at Citadel. "I'm going to ask you one more time, have you seen Flint?"

They stared, rather surprised by the tone in Spencer's voice, he hadn't gone out of his way to be friendly when they arrived, but he wasn't rude or mean. They figured he was one of those strong, silent types, not so silent right now.

"Leroy and Spencer have some history," Travis nodded at them.

"History," Trevor scoffed. "Leroy decided to paint graffiti on Spencer's hover."

"The one thing you don't do is mess with Spencer's ride." Aurelius nodded.

"And we missed that?" Wes looked at Paul who was watching Spencer and Leroy, neither one backing down.

The gnome does realize that Spencer makes at least five of him, right? Cole didn't want to ask out loud, not that any of them could blame him nor argue with his assessment. Leroy still sat on the bar stool and Spencer still towered at least 5 feet over him. But they had to hand it to the gnome, he didn't look the least intimidated.

"Spencer," Jeff spoke up and after a moment or two, Spencer backed up but kept his eyes on Leroy who turned away from Spencer looking up at Jeff, the same standoffish attitude written all over him as he waited for Jeff to speak up. Jeff tossed a golden coin onto the bar counter in front of Leroy. "We're looking for Flint, Leroy. Help us bring him in before he hurts others."

Leroy looked down at the coin, lifted it up to his mouth and bit down on it with his blackened teeth, actually breaking a tooth on the coin. His pudgy tongue ran over the broken tooth shard. "You guys are getting desperate if you are bringing out these."

Telara frowned trying to get a look at the coin, it wasn't like any money she had ever seen.

"Have you seen him, talked to him or heard anything about his whereabouts?" Jeff asked him then jerked back when Leroy flung the coin back at him.

"You think this is worth betraying the only Hunter who cared about us out here? He's in hiding because of you and even if I knew where he was, I wouldn't tell you." Leroy glared at Jeff. "He has earned our allegiance time and again when Sanctuary and the Hunters turned their backs on us."

"Everyone here wanted to live outside Arion control, you knew the risks," Travis told him from his position beside the bar.

Telara looked at Pam and the other Arions from Sanctuary, Pam was watching the exchange between the gnome and the Hunters but keeping silent. Donny and Chez both were watching the exchange as well while Gabe and Zeke were canvassing the room, their hands close to their Crims.

"So, you turn your back when the Shadows attack!" Leroy accused him, pointing a pudgy finger at all of them. He stopped when he saw Telara and the other Guardians, giving them a curious look.

Jessie moved in front of him blocking his view of them. "It wasn't like that; we came and chased the Shadows from here."

"Too late!" Leroy spat at him.

"We came as soon as we were notified that the Shadows were attacking." Trevor moved forward. "You refused any of our security measures that could have alerted us as soon as the Shadows crossed the border."

Leroy harrumphed. "We refuse to be under your thumb or be under any obligation to you, didn't mean we should expect to have our buildings destroyed and people taken."

"If we hadn't come, the damage would have been ten times worse," Aurelius defended. "We defeated them!"

"Then left us to rebuild on our own!" Leroy glared at him.

I.Q. turned, looking at the rest of them, his expression gone slack.

Am I the only one confused with this conversation? He asked.

Nope! The mental response was unanimous.

"We were told to leave!" Trevor held up his hands in frustration, not that Telara could blame him.

"You didn't try to stay either. It was Flint who came back and helped us rebuild as well as bringing food and supplies to those that were in need."

"Do you really think Stazi didn't know what Flint was doing? That she didn't authorize it?" Jeff asked Leroy, whose expression was still closed to him, as if not listening to anything that was being said.

"Flint is working for the ones who attacked your home!" Aurelius's voice showed his frustration.

"Says you." Leroy shrugged.

Trevor countered, "Says the facts!"

His mind is closed, Tia spoke, but her gaze was on Leroy who kept sending sidelined glances their way, when Travis or one of the other Hunters weren't standing in his way.

He is being stupid. Cole looked irritated and they couldn't blame him for being aggravated but it was Vanna who decided to give the other side.

He is just being loyal to someone who helped him and everyone else here, came the response from their little pacifist, who had to see the good in everyone.

Leroy clambered down from the bar stool walking away with one last parting shot, "No one here is interested in your facts." The door to the tavern slammed in the quiet room.

Jeff turned to look at the barkeep behind the bar counter, tossing him the coin that landed on top of the counter. "If you hear anything, contact us." The short, stubby male whose skin looked grayish stared back at him with a stony expression.

He turned away looking around the bar then looked at

Spencer, "Any other leads for us to follow?" Spencer gave a slow shake of his head and Jeff sighed.

"How can they protect someone who turned his back on them?" Chance asked out loud, his frustration at what they just saw was evident in his voice and expression.

"Flint was well liked," Aurelius told him.

"Still is from what I see," Vanna spoke up, staring at him with almost a challenge in her posture causing Aurelius and a few of the other Hunters' expressions to harden.

Jeff shook his head at them and looked at Vanna, "You have to understand, it isn't just that Flint was one of us Hunters, he was family to us. He was one of the best Hunters and for him to switch allegiance was shocking." He looked over to where Spencer stood with Pam, Donny, Wes and Paul were all standing.

During all their adventures Telara did think it was weird that their friends from their Sanctuary were rather silent and letting others lead.

Gage let the leaders in Alaska lead, Chance pointed out to Telara's thoughts, reminding them all that their thoughts were rarely private anymore.

This feels different, his brother spoke up giving side glances towards Pam and the other Arions, trying to be inconspicuous but in reality, it didn't matter. It seemed the Arions weren't paying the Guardians any mind. Telara nodded in agreement with Chad, this did feel different and they couldn't understand why. Pam was barely talking to them and since they had become friends, Telara didn't know what that felt like. She had a feeling it wasn't personal but she couldn't help taking it a bit personally, she missed her friend.

We don't know the story, Tia reminded her and she sighed with a very imperceptive nod.

Maybe tonight when we get back to the Citadel and relax in the Love Goddess's love nest. Telara tried to hold back the chuckle at Cole's quip, although she wasn't sure why. None of the Arions were looking at them, it wasn't like there was anyone feeling left out of the conversation this time.

"So, what could the Shadow Master have promised Flint to make this glorified soul of a man turn on his friends and beliefs?" Chad asked. Everyone around him stilled at his question and his eyes darted all around him. "Did I say something wrong?"

Jeff just gave a shake of his head and answered his first question but ignored the second one. "We won't know until we ask him."

"We never find out what the Shadow Master promises," Trevor spoke up.

"What about rogues in the past? Surely they have told you?" Chance asked, looking around at them.

It was Jeff who gave a shake of his head, as if saying the words was too hard.

"Why?" Telara asked, dreading the answer.

But no answer came, the expressions on the Hunters' and Arions' faces became even more somber, not a one looked at them as the mood darkened even more. Telara swallowed hard as they all realized how serious the stakes were.

"Oh." Such a small word with such a depth of meaning as they followed Jeff and the others out of the tavern that they didn't even know the name of. Looking back, Telara saw that the coin was no longer on the counter but the stone man was no longer there either.

12

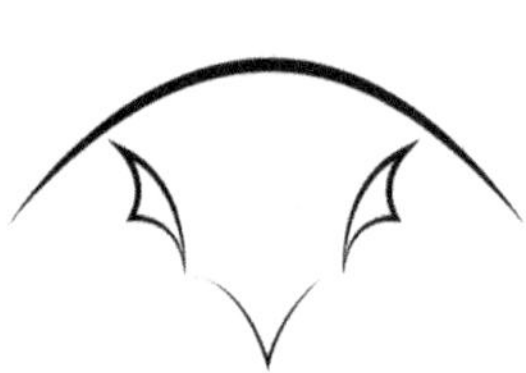

WALKING TOWARDS THE HOVERS, Telara jerked when Tia nudged her none too gently. Looking over where Tia was motioning to with a jerk of her head, Telara saw the hag from inside climbing on what looked like a black rock. The others turned when they realized that Telara and Tia weren't with them, Jeff frowned then looked over to where they were staring.

Everyone turned to look and as they all watched as the rock moved beneath the hag. Dark legs appeared beneath the rock as a small head appeared with two antennas. Tia and Telara looked at each other as they realized what they were seeing was another Shadow creature, this one resembled a pill bug. The pill bug reared up and then shot off faster than any creature they had ever seen.

"Let's go!" Jeff shouted but everyone was already running to their hovers as they followed the hag who was so far ahead of them, Telara worried they wouldn't be able to find her.

Great, another Shadow groupie, Cole grumbled.

Did Zach say anything about a hag working with the Shadows? Chance asked Telara who just shook her head, no longer caring if the others noticed they were speaking mentally. They were so out of the loop and all of them were getting frustrated with being in the dark, they were beginning to wonder if they would be able to change their destiny. It was as if everything they learned and everything they did only brought more questions, but few answers.

Every set of Guardians that came before them died when they faced the Shadow Master; they were supposed to be different. They were doing things differently than the others; they grew up outside of the Sanctuary and they lived outside the Sanctuary. They mingled with the Arions and they even got to meet Rogue Hunters, but yet it felt as if they weren't any further than when they first came to Sanctuary, not even knowing they were the Guardians of Sanctuary.

In the distance they saw a dark figure that the hag was racing to, as they got closer, they realized it was a building, a house to be exact. Although the closer they got they saw the house looked like one you would see in a horror movie. Shutters hung by one hinge, paint peeled and wooden slats were missing or on the ground. There were some trees around the home that went with the horror film atmosphere, dead and black with an eerie feeling.

There was no driveway or even a road that led to the house, looking around the area they saw nothing but emptiness. They were practically in the middle of a grassy field with nothing around them, no roads, no power lines, no nothing.

They climbed off their hovers and looked around for the Shadow pill bug but he was nowhere to be seen.

"I have a bad feeling about this." Chad looked around, his hands unconsciously rubbing his arms as if he was chilled in the summer air.

"You can stay out here if you want," Trevor told him, grabbing some crystal trinkets from his bag on his hover. "But we are going in, that is what Hunters do." The meaning in his words were clear and also enough to stiffen Chad's spine as they all started walking to the house.

"Let's hope this porch holds all our weights," Chad spoke, his voice low, not wanting Trevor to take another jab at him. Telara doubted they were the only ones holding their breath as they stepped onto the weathered, splintered wood on the steps of the porch. Mainly because of the fact that no one remarked on Chad's words.

The floor groaned with each step they took but they tried to not to think about that, their lair back at home wasn't in the best condition but was a mansion compared to this place.

Wonder if this place has a basement? Cole looked at them.

Why don't you go find out? Tia grinned at him.

"No way!" Cole said out loud, which considering everything was quiet in this abandoned house as they were all moving soundlessly through the home, sounded like a bullhorn around them. The Arions and Hunters turned to stare at him, Pam shook her head at them as she realized they had been speaking via their mindspeak.

Telara mouthed sorry to her even though she didn't think they should be sorry for speaking silently when no one was really talking to them. Jeff and Spencer frowned at them, so they went quiet as Trevor moved to the center of the hallway they were standing in, placing a silver metal disk that sparkled with what only could be crystal essence on the floor.

They stood there waiting for something to happen, not really sure what though. When nothing happened and Trevor picked up the disk placing it back in his pouch they looked around. "Was something supposed to happen?" Cole asked.

Trevor grinned at him but Jeff was the one who spoke, "Mess with them later Trevor, not now." Jeff looked at them. "If there had been Shadows, the disk would have gone off but it seems the house is Shadow free."

"What about the pill bug the hag was riding?" I.Q. asked.

"Did you see it enter the house?" Travis asked him.

I.Q. snorted. "I didn't even see the hag enter the house."

"Exactly," Trevor spoke up.

"So, how do we know she's here then?" Telara frowned.

"We don't." Jeff lifted a shoulder as he pulled out something that finally looked familiar to them, a Crim. "But this is the only place for miles and miles, so we check it out."

"What is this place?" Vanna asked, looking at the broken frames that hung from nails in the walls of the hallway, some still had dusty looking pictures of people that were probably long gone in them.

"Your guess is as good as ours," Aurelius told her as he turned into a room on their right, his Crim in his hand as well but just like Jeff it was in relaxed form. "I would get out your Crims, just in case," he told them.

Looking around, they saw that everyone else had their Crims in hand as they moved cautiously into other rooms that were as empty as the kitchen the Guardians had followed Aurelius into.

"Of course, the room he chose would be the kitchen." Chad quipped, then pressed his lips together quickly, sure a rebuke would be coming for him joking while they were in this situation.

"Didn't take long for them to get you figured out, man," Trevor chuckled as Aurelius shrugged.

"I like my food. I won't deny that," he responded.

"What's that?" Vanna pointed to an oval-shaped object on the floor. When they moved closer, it looked like a leather strap that was curled into the shape.

Pam was the one who moved forward and picked it up, her eyes wide as she looked at Jeff who nodded. They looked at each other then back at those two. "What?"

Pam actually answered them, "It's Flint's."

"So, he is or was here then?" Cole asked and Pam gave an uncertain nod.

"Either that or it was placed to distract us," She looked around the room, on the west side of the wall a bookshelf had been built into the wall with books still there although beneath the dust and cobwebs you couldn't tell what was written on the spines. "The hag might have warned him."

Out of the corner of her eye, Telara saw Trevor give a grin she knew from experience with Cole and Chad meant nothing but trouble. He pulled out a smaller disk than he had before, one that resembled the one that had floated Chad out of the swampy water before. He tossed it at Cole's feet then stood back his eyes bright.

Telara frowned as nothing happened. "That was a bit anticlimactic," she told Trevor, whose eyes went wide and his face paled a bit. She gave him a funny look then looked over at Aurelius whose expression mirrored Trevor's. "What's going on?"

"That was an aerodisk, your friend should be at least three feet off the ground right now," Trevor told her as his grip on his Crim tightened and all of the others had gone into defense mode, their postures alert and eyes watching everything.

"I don't get it, so it was a dud." Telara looked around but still wasn't sure what was going on.

"It wasn't a dud," Trevor told her as he moved cautiously towards the door.

"Then why didn't it work?" Telara started to get confused and could feel confusion emanating from her friends as well. They could feel the change in I.Q.'s confusion when he spoke, they could feel it clearing up as he realized why everyone was on high alert.

"There is something in this house preventing the disk from working," he spoke softly, his hand with his watch straightening as the Hunters nodded moving out into the hallway and down the hall, slowly and cautiously. "Then that means there could be another reason the Shadow detector hadn't lit up." More nods and that was when they realized what the alarm was.

There could be Shadows in this house, could even be the Shadow Master or the female in the cloak who could control the Shadows. They weren't sure which was worse, considering they had never met the Shadow Master but had come face to face with her.

"Crims at the ready everyone," Jeff told them quietly as they continued towards the door. "Not sure if they will work with whatever is smothering the detectors and aero disks, but better to have them at the ready."

"Our Crims are always at the ready," Telara told him as her arm with the Rotary on it was bent out in front of her. Jeff had a confused look but shrugged as they finally reached the porch and were out of the house.

Although what awaited them outside was just as chilling as the empty rooms and hallway they vacated. Even more so. There beneath one of the horror movie trees stood a tall male, at least six feet or more, staring at them with a mocking expression on his face.

"Flint," Pam breathed from beside Telara. Even without Pam's acknowledgement, they would have recognized him from the picture on the screen that Stazi had shown them during their briefing. His dark eyes moved to where Pam stood, an emotion they couldn't define crossed his face but was gone just as quick.

The hag was there as well, sitting on the Shadow pill bug but the most chilling thing were all the Shadows that stood there as well. Minions bent over with barely human faces, their clawed hands swaying slowly in front of them. Other Shadows that resembled human-like trolls several feet taller than the Minions standing there as well. Then you had the Shadows that had the shapes of big cats or even big bears that were moving back and forth watching them closely.

"There has to be thirty to forty Shadows," Tia spoke, her arm bracelets moving down her arm, her whip forming in her hand.

Travis shrugged. "Yeah, the odds are definitely in our favor." He gave a grin that belied the situation they were in.

"Are you crazy?" Chad asked as they watched Travis' Crim formed into a heavy club with a crystal blade through the tip.

"I think that answers your question." Telara turned back to the scene in front of her as Flint moved forward, his gaze no longer on Pam but on Jeff who was on the top step of the porch, his Crim turning into a heavy looking mallet with a golden metal handle about two feet long with a metal head with yellow crystal twined within.

Flint shook his head, addressing Jeff, "Man, you are too predictable. I don't need to be warned of what you're doing, I already know what you are going to do before you even know."

Jeff twirled the mallet in his hand, the crystals glowing. "How about you step away from your new friends and come closer, let's see how predictable I am then." The hardness in voice showed in his expression.

Spencer's Crim turned into a two-sided battle axe that he gripped tightly, watching Flint, the hag and the Shadows.

Flint just laughed and shook his head, "Sorry man, I got plans that don't include sparring with you. Besides, we know how it ends, just like always with you on your ass." Flint turned to where a Shadow horse like creature appeared and mounted up. He turned and gave them all a salute before galloping off, the hag following leaving them there with the Shadows who were starting to move towards them.

"Flint!" Jeff yelled but the horse nor the pill bug slowed as they disappeared from their sight.

13

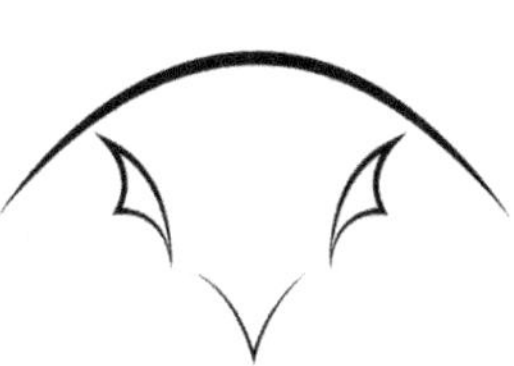

"GET READY," Jeff told them as he twirled his mallet, moving down the steps watching the Shadows moving towards them, growling and grumbling with each movement.

Travis grinned tossing his club from hand to hand, turning to Trevor, he taunted, "Loser takes the winner's janitorial rounds."

Trevor's Crim twirled between his fingers and started growing until he was gripping a pole in his hand that had a crystal blade that arched back. "Dude, better get your mop and bucket ready." With that, Trevor leaped off the porch, running towards the Shadows.

"Hey!" Travis yelled out, jumping down from the porch, swinging his club at the nearest Minion, who let out a strangled yell when the point of the crystal blade connected with its shoulder, knocking it back. "I didn't give the signal yet, man!"

Trevor twisted in time to avoid the claws of a Shadow big cat, his pole swinging, the blade connecting with the arm of the cat, who let out a painful mewl. "If I waited for you, I would be gray and wrinkled. You're getting slow in your old age."

Travis snorted barely dodging one of the troll-like Shadows, he turned with his club but before he could take out the troll Jessie leapt over the troll, his Crim separating into two daggers that sank into the shoulders of the troll who screamed out in pain.

Travis frowned at him. "Whoa brother, that one was mine!"

Jessie landed on his feet shrugging with a grin. "Not anymore."

"Jessie!" Trevor shouted, but the bear leapt up and landed on Jessie, who hit the ground so hard, his daggers fell from his hands.

"Not my brother." Travis swung his club on the bear's head while Trevor swung his pole blade, hitting the bear on his backside.

"Noooo!" Vanna shrieked, jumping off the porch. "They could be friends." Travis and Trevor ignored her as they kept fighting the bear-like Shadow, keeping its massive jaw from biting down on Jessie's throat and pulling him into the shadows around them. If that were to happen, they would lose Jessie.

Vanna, be careful, Telara told her, jumping down with others to join the battle. *They need to keep the Shadows from pulling him into the shadows.*

They understood how Vanna felt, the image of Gage laying on the ground during the big battle at Sanctuary still haunted them all the time. The guilt of thinking that Gage was taken by the Shadows and was lost to them was nothing compared to finding out that the Shadows they were fighting were actually lost friends the Shadow Master had turned into Shadow creatures.

But they still hadn't figured out about the shape shifting Shadows from Alaska that disappeared rather than revealed a person or mythical that had been changed. As they thought about that the bear changed his shape to a snake that wrapped its tail around Jessie's leg and started to slither away dragging him.

"No!" Travis, who had been tossed back by the bear, tried to jump up and run after his brother.

A bright flash shot right by them almost blinding them as it hit the snake who screamed out in pain, letting go of Jessie who flipped back away from the snake, his Crims appearing in his hands, ready to battle but the snake disappeared.

"What the hell was that?" Travis turned where I.Q. stood with his bow, aiming at another Shadow letting loose another electric bolt.

Cole twirled his fiery nunchucks, knocking a troll-like Shadow from who was reaching for Chez, who had just thrown his boomerang Crim at a big cat Shadow that was changing shape to a big bird reaching for Spencer who was fighting with a troll-like Shadow.

Aurelius swung his forked prong sword connecting with a minion who jerked back with a screech, the intricacy on his sword reminded them of what you would see in a fantasy RPG game.

"Telara!" Tia screamed, as the snake that had disappeared after attacking Jessie sprung from the shadows and coiled around Telara's legs and arms so fast she couldn't react. Her body fell back, gripped tightly in the snake's coils, her head hit the ground with a thud. The world around her spinning as the snake tightened its grip around her making it hard for to breath.

"No!" She wasn't sure who screamed, the yells and shouts were starting to blend together. She could feel the Shadow snake moving across the ground, heading to the closest shadow, she was sure. Bright flashes of light lit up around her, dirt flying as I.Q. sent electrical bolts that the snake kept avoiding.

"Don't let it get near a shadow!" Pam's panicked voice

broke through the fog in her head. She tried to move her arm so she could use her Rotary but the coils were too tight.

She was being dragged to a nearby shadow she was sure, her vision starting to blur so that there was nothing for her to concentrate on, anything to give her some sort of control over her situation. Everything felt as if it was moving in slow motion, then the whole world stopped. The snake's body that was coiled around her disappeared and she felt the ground beneath her and her vision started to clear.

There, before her with his icy sword in the ground where only moments ago was the snake, was Chad staring at her with wide, panicked eyes. The others ran up to her helping her up, all as pale as Chad as they dusted grass and dirt off of her.

"Are you okay?" Tia asked her, eyes bright with unshed tears. Telara nodded, not trusting her voice right now, her throat was sore and her body felt bruised but she refused to let them treat her as an invalid just because she was stupid enough to let a Shadow get too close.

"Glad to see you standing, how about some help over here," Jeff shouted at them, taking out another Shadow with his club.

Telara looked at the ground where the snake had been only moments before. "You don't think-?"

"No, I don't," Vanna told her, surprising them all. "If it had been someone, there would have been a body there, of that, I'm sure."

They nodded, refusing to think anything else as they rushed to help Jeff, Pam and the others who were fighting.

With a flick of her wrist, the Rotary formed into a thick whip that knocked one of the minions away from Jeff. The minion screamed and ran for a shadow but Tia was twirling her whip in the air, kicking up a lot of wind in the process. With a flick of her whip, she knocked the minion away from the shadow it was heading for. The minion rolled and stopped right at Vanna's feet, with just a touch of her staff the minion let out a scream as the world around it glowed revealing a small petite little blond girl unconscious on the ground.

Vanna grinned at them. "I still got it!"

"Mica would be proud." Tia nodded, speaking of the Paladin Vanna had freed from being a tree in the yard of the pixie princess while they were in Alaska, the only Paladin they liked. Kull, another Paladin, they had rescued from being cursed as a dragon when they discovered the town of Lapros that was cursed in time by the Gods. While Mica had been thankful and seemed helpful, Kull needed an attitude adjustment.

Chance joined the fray, his flail connecting with the head of one of the troll-like shadows. Water splattered all around them and the troll fell face first into the ground. Before it could rise up, Vanna leapt through the air, landing on its back, her staff pressed against it. More bright light and she found herself on the back of an unconscious dark-skinned guy who looked like he could be a quarterback.

"Now, we could use one of those." Trevor nodded at Vanna's staff.

Vanna smiled and shrugged. "I don't think it will work for you like it does me."

Trevor shrugged. "Was worth a shot."

Vanna laughed and Gabe frowned at Trevor, pulling small smiles from Telara, Tia and the other Guardians while Vanna seemed oblivious as she looked around at the dissipating battle around them.

Telara looked up at Jeff and Pam. "Where are the other Shadows?"

Pam nodded towards Vanna, "Just like always as soon as they see her healing the other Shadows they start to scramble away."

I.Q. grinned as he walked over to them, "That's our mother

nature," he said proudly, then he looked over at Telara. "How are you?"

She gave a shrug, feeling self-conscious that she let one of the Shadows get the better of her. "I'm fine." She started rubbing her arms, already feeling the tenderness from the snake's grip.

"We could get you back to the med unit, we have the best of the best when it comes to a medical facility," Travis told her, but she shook her head.

"I'm fine, I promise." She smiled at the Hunters, who were watching her closely.

That smile is too bright for me to take it seriously, Tia spoke via their mental bond, with everyone else giving their mental agreement.

Telara flinched as Tia's voice sounded louder than normal in her head then sighed, *Please, guys, let this drop. I feel foolish enough as is.*

This isn't your fault, Vanna protested. *If you need medical help, you need to say something.*

I will, I promise. Telara smiled, trying to hide another grimace, then gave a pointed look at Pam who was staring at them while the other Arions and Hunters helped up the few that Vanna was able to heal. The mental chatter seemed to be taking more energy from her, something that hadn't happened before.

"Sorry." They all spoke at the same time but Pam shook her head with a smile.

"I'm just glad you're okay," she told Telara, who gave her a mock surprised look. Then Pam's eyes twinkled, "You wouldn't believe the paperwork involved when a Guardian gets taken."

"Hey!" Telara protested and they all laughed, feeling more normal again.

Travis and Trevor walked up to them with matching grins that felt out of place right now. "We got a med unit coming to pick up the survivors and take them back to RC."

"So, what were you guys talking about before the fight?" Chad asked, but they looked confused. "Something about janitorial duty and winners and losers?"

"Yeah." Travis turned to Trevor who pulled out an electronic pad that resembled a smartphone. They watched as Travis did the same, holding them both out they looked at each other. "Ready?" Trevor nodded and simultaneously they touched the black screens. The faces lit up and numbers appeared in the air over the screens.

"Yes!" Trevor shouted, grinning at the number ten hovering over his pad while a number nine could be seen over Travis'.

"No way," Travis exclaimed then he turned to Jessie, who shook his head. "This is your fault, man. If you hadn't let that silly little snake sneak up on you, I wouldn't have had to try to save your sorry ass."

"You aren't putting this one on me," Jessie told him, walking away.

Trevor grinned. "That makes two weeks of armory cleaning."

"Yeah, yeah," Travis grumbled, swiping his thumb across the screen, the number disappearing and the screen going black once again.

"They take bets on who takes out the most Shadows," Aurelius explained as they stared at the dejected Travis who was walking away, still yelling at his brother, while Trevor looked like the cat who ate the canary. "Loser takes the winner's chores."

Telara and the other Guardians laughed. Tia looked over at Chad and Cole. "I can see you two doing that."

Vanna's head whipped around glaring at them, they both held up their hands. "We didn't say that and we wouldn't."

Her eyes narrowed. "Make sure you don't."

Aurelius laughed. "Flint is gone and our leads have gone

cold, so we are heading back to freshen up, then head to the Crystal Con. You guys interested in joining us?"

"Yeah!" The decision was unanimous and Aurelius laughed as they headed to their hovers. The med units had arrived and were taking care of the few survivors Vanna was able to save.

14

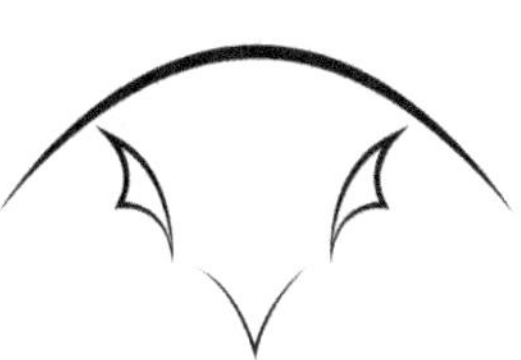

"ARE you ready to put your skills to the test?" Drago was standing center stage in the middle of the vast room where the heart of the Con took place. The day before, the room was full of tables with stars and artists of all sorts there to sign books, prints or whatever their fans wanted. Now there were still tables, although not as many, but they lined the outside walls while a black curtain wrapped around some type of exhibit in the center of the room. The same black curtain that was behind Drago on his stage.

Kashan, Drago's best bud and a General in Drago's sector, joined him on the stage. The room erupted in loud cheers and applause as soon as he stepped up on the stage. He was not as tall as Drago but with skin just as dark and a smile that set many groupie girls all dreamy-eyed. During a live podcast with Drago, Kashan and some other players in their sector, Steve, an officer in their sector, told Kashan he was the reason for all the strict procedures they had for anyone joining their sector. Kashan smirked, remarking that Steve was jealous. To Steve's credit, he didn't deny it, he admitted it right out.

"Get out those Crystal cards, people, and get your avatars

ready!" Kashan's voice echoed all around the room. "It's time for the announcement you have all been waiting for, the big event that we have been setting up for the past year. Who in this room would love to see the best game in the year played in 3D?"

The room erupted around them while Drago and Kashan were up on the stage moving their hands in circles getting the crowd to scream louder. Telara grinned at Tia as they sat back a bit while the guys, even I.Q., were shouting with the rest. Pam sat back with them while Donny, Zeke, Gabe and Chez were shouting as well. Wes, Paul, Jayne and Lucy sat back, watching the scene around them. The Hunters were there, well most of them.

James and Mark were nowhere to be seen when they got back from the horror movie house, when they asked where they were Stazi told them Lucius sent them to meet up with James' brothers. Chad had to act shocked that James had brothers, Travis snorted at him. "What, you don't think any of us who work with Sanctuary can have family?"

Chad tried to apologize, but Travis wouldn't let him, they weren't sure if he was messing with him or if Chad had actually offended him. This group was different than any they had met, the way they talked to each other at times made it so you weren't sure if they even liked each other. Of course, Travis was still sore at losing to Trevor, so that could have something to do with it as well.

"Everyone in this room will be the first to see the next evolution of Crystal Paladins, no longer will they be stuck on a flat TV screen. Now you will feel as if you are a part of their world, behind this curtain you will step into the world of the Crystal Paladins. Are you ready?"

Telara could barely hear with all the shouts, and the floor vibrated from the stomping and jumping of everyone at Drago's words as he worked the stage along with Kashan. Separate,

Drago and Kashan were forces to be reckoned with, but together they were more formidable than any force of nature. It was so loud, Telara's ears started ringing, her head felt fuzzy again, almost like she was back in the Shadow snake's clutches.

Tia frowned at her, mouthing, "Are you okay?" Telara gave an unconvincing nod, one she knew her friend wasn't buying.

If you need to leave, we can go outside. Tia spoke through their mind link, the best way to be heard in this room. Telara blanched as her head started to buzz loudly as if thousands of bees had taken root inside. If not for Pam, she would have fallen over, the noise making her off balance. Both Tia and Pam looked concerned but she just shook her head at them, she didn't want to ruin the day for the guys. Besides, she was looking forward to seeing what was behind the curtain as well.

"What is the pass phrase?" Drago asked the room and the reply was deafening.

"Don't die!"

With those words, the curtain fell to the ground and before them they saw at least a hundred or more black consoles making a perfect box around the center of the room. In the center were poles with solar panel-looking gadgets as well as picnic table sized panels along the floor with wires and plugs all around.

"After Christmas we picked one hundred and fifty players to be a part of this exciting new adventure, you know who you are!" Kashan walked excitedly along the stage. "You got the invite and I hope you didn't toss that invite away because that invite is your ticket here!" Kashan shouted pointing to the center of the room where the lights came on from the solar panels, right above the table sized panels images came alive. It was one of the cut scenes from their game. "You will be one of the very first to play the interactive Crystal Paladin player versus player war. The winner will win a trip to Florida and the headquarters of the Crystal Paladin world."

Everyone in the room started rummaging through purses, backpacks and jean pockets for the invite.

"Those who didn't get an invite will have front row seats to the biggest gaming event of the year, possibly the entire decade!" Drago's deep voice echoed around the room as benches rose from the floor around the console pit in the center of the room. "So, let's do this! Ticket holders, line up and present your ticket, only those with tickets will be allowed in the pit. Everyone else go find yourself a seat with a good view, you won't want to miss this!"

Everyone but Pam, Jayne, Lucy and Stazi walked up to the stage with their tickets. Even Vanna had a ticket and was looking forward to bringing her avatar to life in front of everyone. Pam and Stazi sat down in the front row, their gazes taking in everything around them like the leaders they were, Jayne and Lucy were chatting like best friends gesturing around them grinning and laughing.

"Hey, look!" Turning towards the direction Chance was pointing in they saw Brian and Levi on the stage talking with Drago and Kashan.

"Look!" Trevor pointed towards the pit where black screens rose in front of the consoles, making it hard to see the other players. Walking around the consoles shaking hands of players and nodding were actors dressed up like the Paladins.

A tall male dressed in the fiery red and yellow cloak with golden accents that the Crystal Paladin Brakus wore was shaking the hand of a slender blond who was almost hyperventilating. A slap on her arm had Telara turning with a frown as Vanna kept hitting her to get her attention. "Look! Look! Look!" Vanna's tone rose in her excitement as they saw the green Paladin Tarmyr walk with the grace of royalty.

Telara laughed, handing her ticket to Drago who smiled down at her, winking as he took the ticket, punching out the crystal logo in the corner before handing it back to her. "Don't forget about the after party," he told her.

"I won't," She promised him with a smile, laughing as Tia and Vanna both made swooning motions.

"I bet Adam wouldn't be happy to hear you're flirting with Drago," Cole said as he walked by grinning.

Telara frowned at him. "One, I wasn't flirting, and two, me and Adam aren't dating."

"Well, you could be." Tia shrugged as they descended the steps down into the pit to find their console.

Telara snorted at that, "Exactly how would that work when I would have to explain why I'm canceling a date to fight Shadows?" Effectively silencing her friends, she found her console and pulled out her USB card with her avatar and card information.

Sorry, Tia said with others echoing her. Telara blanched as the words set her mind into a dizzy spin like earlier. She felt their concern but shook her head, she didn't think she could handle another mental conversation right now. She looked into the crowd meeting Pam's gaze. The look in Pam's eyes told her that she caught the reaction and was suspicious. Telara tried to give her an encouraging smile but it felt wrong so she just turned back to the console waiting for the signal to insert their USB.

A giant image of Drago appeared before them all, torso and head only floating above the panels. The floor of the panels still had the scenery from the game, multicolored crystals with flora of all shapes and colors that grew in the world of the Crystal Paladins. The scenery was from the land of Taron, the starter land in the Crystal Paladin world. Here the physical labor working class like farmers, tailors and others lived. Everyone started here as a physical laborer and their goal was the great city of Arion.

After discovering that residents of Sanctuary were called Arions, short for Sanctuarians, Cole started pointing out the similarities but stopped after his confrontation with Kull in Alaska. Now, he rarely remarked on any of the similarities between their new life and everything they learned. His silence made those similarities louder to the others, though they tried to not think too much about it knowing how it bothered him.

"Get those USBs ready!" Drago's voice boomed around them.

Brian's face appeared with that red fez of his and contagious smile. "Show us those avatars!" His voice not as deep as Drago's but it was heard clearly.

The area in front of them lit up with visions of all types of avatars. Telara's rose in front of her and her breath caught at the sight of her. She had chosen the warrior pixie model with bright purple hair that flowed around her and matched the dull purple skin with deep purple eyes. Her model crouched low, looking around, always on alert and ready for battle. She had chosen the profession of a thief and assassin. Next to her, Tia stood with regal grace, alabaster skin and silver hair flowing around her and the gown she wore. Tia had chosen the profession of a Regent, saying she learned how to be diplomatic from dealing with Cole all the time.

Cole's avatar was easy to find as he stood tall with fiery red hair, towering over many others. He had chosen a warrior profile and profession, in his avatar's hand was clutched his sword and shield. The symbols on his shield showing the many victories he had won but still not enough to earn him his way to Arion although both him and Chad had opened up more of the other lands than any of the other Guardians.

Shouts from their right had them looking at an avatar they had never seen before. "Siamese Battle Twins! Siamese Battle

Twins!" came the chant from the stands. Telara turned and saw Stazi, Lucy, and Jayne chanting with their fists in the air while Pam just looked on.

"Yeah!" Telara craned her head past the barrier that made it so it wasn't as easy to see the other players and saw that both Travis and Jessie were at the console that the Battle Twins stood in front of.

"Figures." She laughed looking back at their avatar. From the waist down it looked like one person but the waist up showed two torsos, two sets of arms and two heads. One head had frizzy red hair with glasses while the hair on the other head was clean cut, freckles and pimples could be seen on the frizzy head twin but the other twin's face was clear although they both looked as if they could use some color. The twins started to bang on their chest then one accidentally slapped the other one.

As Telara, Tia, Vanna, Cole, Chad, Chance and I.Q. all watched the twins start fighting each other. One had the other in a stranglehold while the other was yanking at hair. Their attention was diverted when the lights started flashing in front of them.

"Players ready your pets, spells and trap cards!" Kashan was the one speaking this time although he had no image above the pit like Drago and Brian had. "It's time to play Crystal Paladins!"

15

A KEYBOARD ROSE in front of Telara with a controller on the side, a controller she could move to suit her and that controlled her avatar. Her bag of cards with spells, traps and battle pets she could access with the touch of a button. She moved her avatar across the ground and over some boulders as she strategically placed several trap cards to protect her from other players.

With the tap of her thumb, she pulled out her favorite battle pet, a raven that sat on her avatar's shoulder. She was trying to not be so awed by the fact that her avatar was bigger than life size before her. The playing field in the pit had to be the size of the basketball court back at their school but no matter where her avatar moved to, the screen in front of her would follow. Only problem was that doing that moved other players from her view. Hence the trap cards.

She could hear the sounds of battle pets being released and trap cards being set as well as the spell cards being used by master spell casters. She had some spell cards as well but with her avatar being a thief/assassin her strengths were in the trap cards. The sound of the thousand paper cut trap card she placed going off had her turning her avatar to see the image of a large giant avatar with the face of a lion fall to his knees and crumble to the ground before the image dispersed and a buzzer announced another player had been eliminated.

"Man!" They heard the disappointed voice of Jeff and Telara decided she would keep the fact that it was her trap card that had kicked him out of the game to herself.

She had climbed a tree and was about to take out someone who was trying to sneak up Vanna's elven-like avatar who resembled the player, graceful and full of peace and harmony, until you ticked her off. Just as she pulled out her daggers and leapt into the air, a giant hawk appeared before her, its talons open, gripping her avatar in its hold. She groaned as her avatar's image dispersed in many pixels as the buzzer went off, her USB ejecting and her screen lighting up with the words GAME OVER.

She grabbed her USB and stepped back, watching as the battle twins charged a troll-like avatar, taking him down while still shouting at each other. To her left she saw the hooded figure of what resembled a hunter from the game hold out his arm and the hawk perched there, shrinking in size. She turned and saw Aurelius give her a grin before turning back to the game. She laughed and shook her head.

"This way, miss." An attendant opened the gate that kept the audience separated from the players. "You can finish watching from the stands until the final players are done."

Telara joined Pam, Stazi, Lucy, Jayne, Tia, Cole and Jeff who gave her a look that told her he knew whose trap card took him out. She shrugged, that was the name of the game after all.

It was down to Aurelius and another player, everyone else had been eliminated. The Siamese Battle Twins were one of the last ones to go and if they hadn't been bickering, they probably would still be there. It was a good strategy when they weren't actually arguing with each other, the arguing distracted their opponents when they were paying attention. When they weren't, they stepped on a trap card with a hive of crystal bees that took them down.

A drought spell card took out Trevor's imp avatar that kept laying curses of boils and blisters around for others to blunder into. His avatar actually looked as if all moisture was being sucked from its body before it dispersed into many pixels.

Aurelius had sent out his hawk and mighty panther across the field as his avatar moved swiftly to find the other player that seemed to blend in with the darkness. One reverse trap card activated just as his crystal feline stepped on it, putting the feline in its crystal egg and out of the game. Just as they thought Aurelius' hunter had found the other player, a trap card opened up beneath his avatar, the wormhole trap card that sucked his avatar into a wormhole and out of the game.

The whole pit lit up with lights and noises, it had been several long hours but now they had a winner. Aurelius moved to shake the hand of his opponent but as they watched him walk around the consoles they saw him still, turning they couldn't believe who they saw walking with a swagger towards Aurelius with that cocky grin.

"Nothing much has changed; you still rely on those pets of yours. When will you realize it's the traps that win the game?" Flint stood there with that grin while Aurelius stood there his hands clenched into fists.

"Like the one you set up for us … your friends!" Aurelius spoke through his stiff lips.

Flint shrugged. "I knew you wouldn't listen to me and, like I told you, I had plans."

"What plans?" Stazi asked as she and the others moved closer to the barriers, ready to leap over at a moment's notice.

Flint crossed his arms, a triumphant look on his face that didn't waver even when the others had moved forward. "Nuh uh," he told them, gesturing to the crowd around them that screamed and yelled in celebration of the final game. Drago, Kashan, Brian and Levi were calling for both Flint and Aurelius to come up on the stage. They watched helplessly while a stiff-walking Aurelius followed Flint, whose smile hadn't faltered. If anything, it seemed to grow.

"Don't let him out of your sight," Stazi spoke as they moved to stand in the crowd before the stage. "Get the illusion crystals ready, as soon as we have an opening, we need to contain the situation."

Telara watched as the Hunters went from fun loving goofballs to serious warriors, their posture alert and ready as they moved about the room. Each Guardian had their Crims in hand, ready to bring them out and battle. If Flint was here, there was a chance the Shadows and possibly the hag were, too. But why was he here?

Telara fought the urge to ask her friends via their private communication and knew they were hesitant as well. It could be that it was more to do with the loudness of the room but right now she didn't want to take a risk. She needed her wits about her.

DONNY, ZEKE, CHEZ AND SPENCER COVERED ALL THE exits while Gabe, Jayne, Lucy, Wes, Jessie, and Travis walked through the crowds watching as Flint walked confidently with Aurelius to where Drago was clasping their hands in congratulations. Kashan gave them pats on the back as they moved past him to where Brian and Levi were standing their faces beaming.

Aurelius stood there next to Flint with the plaques that Brian and Levi both handed them after handshakes and pictures. Each plaque carried the Crystal Paladins emblem as well as a group picture with all the Paladins in their colorful armor. First place was plainly seen on Flint's while second place was on the one Aurelius held.

"Don't take your eyes off of him," Stazi spoke, her eyes never leaving the stage even as she maneuvered through the crowd gracefully without bumping into anyone.

"You have your plaques, your autographed CD of the music used in the game," Drago's voice boomed around them, Flint held up the CD with a grin while Aurelius stood there more subdued as Dragon continued. "Now for the ultimate prize."

The room erupted with his words as two very elegant females walked out dressed in Paladin finery, bright colorful silk gowns with sleeves that draped down almost to the floor, with multicolored crystals adorning the neck and collars. Their hair pulled back by crystals that flowed down their backs. In their hands were two large envelopes that they handed to Drago, each bowing their head respectfully before turning and walking down the stairs away from the stage.

Drago turned to Flint and Aurelius, first handing Aurelius his envelope then Flint. "In each of these envelopes are packs that contain unique power cards, fashion, mounts and a special crystal card that I will let you both discover." Drago walked the stage as onlookers were quiet so they could hear what prizes were being won.

"The best part is these are tradeable," Kashan said and the crowd started to cheer with this news. He looked at Aurelius who was trying to look excited at the prizes that any player would give their little brother or sister to have in their possession.

Drago walked up to Flint and clasped his shoulder, his voice booming around them, "As the winner you will be given the honor of hosting your very own elite sector alongside me and Kashan." The crowd erupted at that news, there were many sectors in the game but until now there had only been two elite sectors, Drago's and Kashan's. This opened up more opportunities to be accepted into an elite sector, where Flint and Aurelius were being honored with plaques of their achievements. Flint was given the honor of hosting his own sector in Crystal Paladins alongside Drago and Kashan.

Paul and Trevor took points with Pam, Stazi, and Jeff who maneuvered themselves close to the stage watching Flint while Aurelius made sure to keep close to Flint even as others on the stage moved between them. Telara stood back with Tia, Cole, Chad and Chance, but I.Q. and Vanna followed Pam, Stazi and Jeff at a slight distance.

"Think we will end up fighting at the Con?" Tia asked Telara, who watched the stage.

At Tia's words, Telara looked around at the people whose attentions were on the stage as they learned about the new sector and exactly how to join. "Hope not, even with the illusion crystals, it might get hard to conceal everything."

"Then they could see a real crystal battle." Cole shrugged without a grin while he twirled the fiery crystal around his neck with his left hand.

"Let's hope it doesn't come to that," Tia spoke up as her right hand moved to her arm where the arm bracelet glinted in the lights.

Pam turned to them and motioned to the side of the stage where they could see Flint walking calmly down the side stairs after Drago released them telling them not to forget about the after party, Aurelius following him several feet behind. Everyone moved as if in synchronization away from their posts and moving in on Flint who didn't seem to be in any hurry as he moved past tables to the exit.

"Flint!" Jeff shouted at him.

Flint stopped and turned, grinning at everyone that stood there before him, everyone had come together to stop him. He turned to Stazi. "If you missed me that much all you had to do was give me a call, no need to bring out the search party, babe."

Cole's eyes widened looking at Stazi then back at Chance and then Telara, who shook her head. They all heard the underlining insinuation in his words: those two meant something to each other or at least had at one time.

"The guy I miss no longer exists," Stazi told him, her voice tight with emotion but her posture spoke of how alert and ready she was.

"If I thought you would've gone with me, I would've taken you with me. I didn't think you were open to listening," Flint told her, ignoring the others staring at Stazi whose eyes glistened with unshed tears.

"I'm no traitor!" she spoke tightly.

"Neither am I," he told her and sighed. "But you aren't ready to listen." With those words, he turned to leave.

"Flint!" Pam moved forward and they could hear the emotion in her voice, emotion that they didn't understand. Did both Stazi and Pam love Flint?

He stopped and turned, giving Pam a different smile than the one he gave Stazi, his words pulling gasps of shock from Telara and the Guardians. "Hello, little sister." Their gasps pulled his attention from Pam to them and he laughed. "What's wrong, sis, too embarrassed about your big brother to let the new recruits in on the family lineage?"

"Flint, you need to think about what you are doing," Pam told him, moving towards him.

"New recruits?" Chad and Cole looked at each with identical offended looks.

"No, sis, I know exactly what I am doing," Flint told Pam. "You and the others are the ones who need to think about what you are fighting for, or more precisely who you are fighting for."

Pam shook her head at him with a sad expression.

"New recruits?" Chad got louder staring at Flint who barely acknowledged him.

"You guys must be getting desperate bringing new recruits who are unable to control their emotions in the field." Flint chuckled.

"We aren't new recruits." Vanna was the one who stood forward glaring at him. "We are the Guardians and you're a Sally!"

Flint threw his head back, laughing. "I like you!" He pointed at her.

"If you weren't the bad guy, I might take that as a compliment," she told him, crossing her arms.

"Who says I'm the bad guy?" he asked her and she raised a brow.

"Working for the Shadow Master, duh." Her tone showed her annoyance with the discussion.

"I guess it depends on your definition of bad," Flint lifted a single shoulder in a shrug then he lifted two fingers to his temple in a salute. "Would love to stay and chat some more but I have important matters that need my attention." With that, he turned away from them.

"We aren't letting you leave here," Jeff spoke, advancing towards him, but Flint looked over his shoulder with a grin and spoke without slowing his steps.

"You don't want a Crim war here, not with all the normies in the room."

The tightening around Vanna's eyes was the only indication that Flint calling the people normies, a slang word that Arions call the people who live outside of their world, bothered her. Flint, unaware of his offense, kept moving so sure that they wouldn't do anything to stop him when a table slid right in front of him. He turned around with an expression of curiosity and uncertainty.

"Not all of us need our Crims," Telara told him. Her Rotary

glowed brightly on her wrist as Donny, Zeke, Chez and Spencer placed the illusion crystals down around the outside area. Cole moved forward pulling his necklace off and swinging his fiery nunchucks around from hand to hand. Tia with her whip and hair flying from the wind she kicked up as well as Chad with his icy sword in hand and Chance with a watery ball and chain. Flint's eyes narrowed as Vanna moved forward, her belt becoming her nature designed staff and I.Q. pulled back his invisible string on his bow.

"I told you, we're the Guardians," Vanna told him, her chin up and eyes daring him to do anything so she could show how much of a Guardian she was.

To their surprise, Flint raised his hands in surrender, "Who am I to argue with the Guardians?" That truly wasn't the reaction they were expecting as Spencer and Aurelius moved forward, placing crystal cuffs on Flint who watched Vanna, Telara and all the Guardians with an odd expression on his face. Not one Telara was sure she was comfortable with either.

"Let's get him back to the Summit and in custody," Stazi spoke, and now they understood the tightness and odd expressions that both she and Pam had been sharing.

16

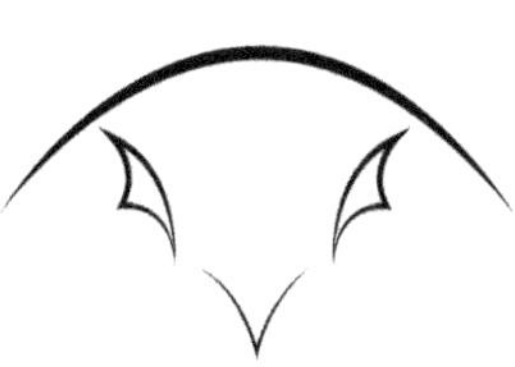

FLINT WAS true to his word; he didn't give them any problem as they took him through the underground passageways to the Citadel. Once again, they climbed into a mining cart although they needed to climb into two separate ones this time, too many for one. They climbed into the same cart as Pam, Stazi, Gabe, Jeff, Spencer and Flint although they noticed how Flint was pushed into the seat closest to the front where Jeff manned the driving seat.

Whenever Telara looked his way, their eyes would meet. He watched her, and she wasn't sure how she felt about it. He chuckled every time she turned away, which would agitate her so she would glare at him, which didn't seem to bother him at all. In fact, if the grin was any indication, it amused him.

This time when the cart hit the surface and rolled towards the barrier that signified the end of the line, they didn't even flinch as the ground opened up and they rode the coaster ride once more. Down past the capital and the living quarters to the ground level, over the water flowing along the rivers from the gentle falls and into several pools, some that glowed green, blue and what other colors they weren't sure of as they saw several smaller cavern openings around them.

"Oh wow!" Chance's low exclamation had them turning away from the colored pools to where he was staring. The building before them was like nothing they had seen before. Unlike the limestone the other buildings in Citadel were built from and into, this building was pure marble and glass. Square pillars rose to meet with the limestone from the cavern around them, archways of pure marble with intricate designs etched into the surface of the several pediments of the grand building.

Marble steps led up to and on either side of the building, where two majestic looking statues stood as if to defend it. A female stood on the left with her head held high, an intricate tiara on her brow, wrapping around coming together side by side. The dress she wore was off the shoulder with sleeves that hung down almost to the ground and wrapped around her hands. In her hands she held a sword that was pointed to the ground below, at the base of the walkway they were now walking across with the water flowing beneath.

The male stood on the right, his eyes staring straight from a helmet that covered his head and part of his face. His armor covered him from his neck down, a shield in one hand while his other hand held a sword tightly in its grasp.

They walked past them both as they moved towards the marble staircase. "Welcome to the Summit," Jeff told them as they moved up the stairs, their eyes staring around in wonder at the new sights.

"Every time we think we have seen the most amazing thing, or have had the most amazing experience, something always proves us wrong." The others nodded in agreement at Vanna's words.

"WILL THIS HOLD HIM?" COLE LOOKED AT FLINT WHO was sitting back on a bench in a holding cell in the Summit. They were told this was where the rogues were brought when they were caught. The holding cells were twelve by twelve with a bench, bed, table and chair. The walls were stone, except for the one facing out into the hallway. That was glass so that if you were standing outside you could see in.

"That's the purpose," Jeff told them as he pushed some buttons on the wall. Flint stared back at them, no remorse or regret on his face, as if he was there talking to friends. "Let's go, we will leave him with his thoughts for a bit. Maybe that will loosen his tongue."

"You really think he'll talk?" Chance asked, looking at Flint who looked more relaxed than any of the rest felt.

It was Stazi who answered, "We can only hope, we need to know why one of ours turned."

"You make it sound as if this is the first time," Vanna frowned. "Isn't that why there are Hunters?"

Stazi sighed, "Rogue Arions yes, but this is the first time a Hunter has ever gone rogue."

"Seriously?" They all turned in surprise but they saw the answer on her face.

"Arions have gone rogue and we have had to chase them down, even some of our own citizens here in Citadel, but never a Hunter, until now." Stazi turned away from staring at Flint. "Let's go."

WALKING DOWN THE STEPS OF THE SUMMIT building, Telara looked back up at the statues; she couldn't describe it but those statues felt familiar to her. Stazi was speaking to Jeff who nodded before he walked away heading towards a smaller building off to the right.

Stazi turned and saw her staring at the statues. "Impressive, aren't they?"

Telara nodded then looked at her. "They are. Who are they?" She didn't want to say anything about them feeling similar before knowing who they are.

Stazi shrugged.

"You don't know anything about the statues built in your own home?" I.Q. asked her.

Stazi gave a slow shake of her head. "They were here long before I was. The Hunters found this place long ago, the Summit and the statues were already here. The Capital and other spires here in Citadel were created by the first Hunters that came here."

Telara looked back up at the statues, into the faces and this time she noticed that the woman was staring at the man while the man was staring out towards the Citadel as if watching over the home of the Hunters. She felt as if there was meaning behind that fact.

A movement to the side had Telara turning to see Pam walking away from the Summit, but it wasn't towards the cart, the building that Jeff went into or even towards Citadel. She was walking off to the left down some more steps then along the stone floor of the cavern.

Telara noticed Stazi talking to Spencer and Gabe. She looked at Tia and her other Guardians; they nodded at her, silently telling her they agreed she should go after Pam. They moved to join Stazi, Spencer and Gabe while she started to follow Pam.

She found Pam in one of the many alcoves they saw during their trip down to the Summit, along the bottom of the cavern. This one had a bluish green river of water that flowed quietly into a pool inside the alcove. In the center was a tree with no leaves that glowed a soft luminescence white, the buds on the tree looked like crystal teardrops along the branches.

"The tree of clarity," Pam spoke softly, startling Telara who had been so captivated by what she saw she forgot she was following Pam.

"Tree of clarity?" Telara turned to see her sitting on a stone bench just inside the alcove. "Can I join you?" She nodded towards the bench where there was room for a few more.

Pam chuckled. "Have I ever been able to stop you?"

"Not really." Telara sat down then looked at the tree. "So, what's the story with this tree?"

"The tree has always been here, the buds that you see that resemble crystal buds have never bloomed," Pam spoke as she stared at the tree.

"Just like the statues?" Pam nodded at Telara's question.

"According to reports from the first Hunters who found Citadel, this area was always here, they were battling some Shadows when they fell right through there." Pam pointed to a pile of rocks on the other side of the pool.

Telara frowned looking around the alcove taking in every detail and realizing something that didn't sit with what she heard, "I don't see any sign there was a battle there." After all, if they fell in the Shadows should have followed and even back in Sanctuary there was a tell-tale sign of the battle at their Bungalow. The Bungalow that was their home in Sanctuary where the Shadows attacked during their original visit to Sanctuary. Vanna's tree still carried marks of that battle, no matter how hard she tried to fix it.

"There wasn't," Pam told her. "When they fell through, the Shadows dispersed and their battle ended."

"What do you mean dispersed?" Telara couldn't understand how Shadows could just disperse in a battle. "How many did they lose?" That was the only time she remembered Shadows dispersing, after they managed to capture some Arions.

"None," was Pam's response. "They discovered that the Shadows couldn't enter this area."

"How?"

Pam shrugged at Telara's question and looked at the tree, "No one truly knows, some believe it is this tree while others believe it is the statues you noticed when we arrived at the Summit." Pam looked around them and sighed, "Could be something in the cavern itself, no one has ever completely figured it out."

"So, why do they call this tree the tree of clarity?" Telara looked over at it. "If it protected this place from the Shadows, you would think it would be called the tree of protection or something."

"Don't you feel it?" Pam asked her but Telara shook her head, not sure what she was supposed to be feeling. "When your mind is unsettled with so much uncertainty and foggy from being full of too much information with no answers, when you are in the presence of this tree it all becomes so clear, you are able to resolve the conflict within."

"Is your conflict resolved?" Telara asked her.

Pam shook her head. "Flint grew up in Sanctuary just as I did, he was leader of the Alpha group with Stazi and Jeff. He taught me everything I know about fighting and being a leader."

"Did Stazi become the leader after he defected?" Telara asked her, but Pam shook her head.

"Flint was offered the position, but he turned it down," Pam said, leaning back against the stone behind them. "After his best friend was taken by the Shadows, he was never the same, he was still one of the best but he started having problems with the authority of Sanctuary. He and Ira had a bad row before he left Sanctuary."

"About what?" Knowing how close Ira was with Pam, that had Telara's attention.

"No one knows," Pam gave a lift of her shoulders. "Neither would speak of it."

Telara wasn't sure what to say to that so she just stared

back at the tree and started to understand what Pam meant when she said the tree was called the tree of clarity. She felt a calmness flow over her, making her wish they could have something like this back home.

"We used to always talk to each other, when I told him about you coming to Sanctuary, he told me I needed to give you a chance and not let our parents' prejudice influence me," Pam revealed, catching Telara's attention at that as her head whipped around to look at Pam, who was staring at the tree.

"Your parents' prejudice?" Telara frowned.

Pam nodded and gave an apologetic smile. "An ancestor of mine was humiliated by your predecessors, they held a position of authority in Sanctuary until he had a run-in with one of the Guardians. He was the head of the Command Center until that day, then he was demoted. He was told it was because he lost sight of the goal of Sanctuary, that he let his pride interfere with his job."

Now Pam's hostility towards them before getting to know them made more sense, they never knew what they did before. She tried to reach out to the others, but her head started to swim when she did.

"You okay?" Pam asked her and she tried to nod, breaking off the attempt at mental communication.

"I'm good," Telara tried to reassure her, but the suspicious look on Pam's face told her she wasn't buying it. She wasn't sure what was happening, since the battle at the haunted house they hadn't been able to speak mentally but right now her friend had bigger problems and that problem was her brother who was sitting in the cell at the Summit. "So, do you know what the fight was about?"

Pam chuckled, looking down at her hands where she was twirling her Crim between her fingers. "Yeah," she said, smacking her lips then looking up towards the roof of the alcove, then tilted her head to look at Telara. "He accused them of letting their egos get in the way of the advantages of working with the Arions. Told them they were signing their own death certificates."

Telara couldn't understand why that would get him fired or even upset the past Guardian. "But he spoke the truth. Why would that get him fired?"

"Guardians come to Sanctuary to train and fight the Magine, that is their only goal. For their service they are treated with reverence while they live and train at Sanctuary," Pam said simply. "At least that is how it always has been and no one argued with it, to do so chanced bringing the wrath of the Gods down on our heads."

Telara snorted. "The Gods who have slept and no one has seen for how long?"

Pam shrugged, "Back then you didn't argue with the status quo; my ancestor did and paid the price."

"Well, don't know if this is any consolation but that Guardian was an idiot." Telara knew she sounded peevish but she couldn't help it, if that Guardian had listened then they might not be going through this now.

"Not really," Pam said then grinned at her. "The only consolation is that I got to know you and the others and am able to call you friends."

Telara's throat constricted at Pam's words, she took a deep breath not wanting her voice to crack when she responded. "That goes both ways."

Pam nodded at her and they went back to staring at the tree before them.

"Flint always believed you guys would come, he never let our parents' prejudice influence his actions. He said you would come and finally defeat the Shadow Master, freeing us all," Pam spoke low. "I never found out what changed his beliefs, how he could follow the one we have fought against all these years."

She hated the pain she heard in her friend's voice, she hated this situation she was in and most of all she was sick and tired of doing nothing while they waited for answers. It was time for them to take the situation in hand. Telara stood up, looking down at Pam who looked startled at her quick movement. "Let's go ask him."

A smile broke out on Pam's face as she rose and nodded.

17

"I STILL THINK he gave in too easy." Jeff was speaking to Stazi, Spencer and Gabe, while Tia and the rest of the Guardians got closer to where they were standing at the steps of the Summit. "Flint isn't one to give up, this doesn't sit well."

"He knew he was facing the Guardians," Cole spoke up, puffing out his chest.

"Yo, how do you walk with that huge head of yours?" Spencer asked him.

"With style." Cole grinned.

"What's going on?" Telara moved closer before Cole ended up upsetting the Hunters that were looking irritated with him.

Stazi turned to them. "Something feels wrong about this, we don't know what is going on in Flint's head and he isn't talking to anyone."

Pam nodded. "I think it's time we ask him and find out what is going on."

"How are you going to do that?" Jeff asked, tilting his head to the side and looking at them.

"We will ask him," Telara stated and Jeff scoffed at her words.

"What do you think we've been doing?" Stazi asked her with an exasperated expression. Telara felt bad for her, it had to be harder on her considering her relationship with Flint.

Pam looked back towards the alcove they had just walked from then back at Stazi. "So, let's go at this from a different angle."

Stazi looked to where Pam was motioning. "Are you crazy?"

Pam looked over at the Guardians. "They might have rubbed off on me."

"You want us to let him out of his cell and take him for a stroll? That is your plan?" Spencer asked as if she had lost her mind.

Stazi was still looking towards the tree of clarity then looked back with a thoughtful look. "Flint always did think the tree helped him think, maybe it could help clear his mind."

"Stazi!" It was Jeff who protested.

"Nothing else is working," Stazi told him.

"But letting him out?" Spencer stared at her. "What if he escapes?"

"It's him against us and the Guardians; he doesn't have the Shadows to help him and besides, are you telling me you don't think your crystal stocks will be able to contain him?" The insulted look on Spencer's face at Stazi's question was almost comical.

"Crystal stocks?" Telara whispered to Pam.

"Kind of like handcuffs except it goes around the waist like a belt, it keeps the person contained but gives them free movement," Pam told her.

"Contained?" I.Q. looked confused.

Spencer held up a remote in his hand and tossed it to Pam. "It will keep him contained, I don't create anything less than perfect."

"And you call me egotistical?" Cole snorted.

"It isn't egotistical, just facts." Spencer stared at him.

"You guys create your own crystal pieces?" Vanna asked and Spencer shrugged.

"I was Gamma when I was at Sanctuary, I brought my expertise with me when I joined the Hunters."

"Let's do this, not like we have anything to lose," Stazi shrugged and turned to Spencer. "Bring him out." Turning to Pam, "Who do you want with you."

Pam gave an apologetic look to her, "I think it would be best if it is just me and the Guardians."

Stazi nodded, "I don't like it but I agree, he was always fascinated with the coming of the Guardians." She nodded. "Go, Spencer will bring him to you."

FLINT STOOD THERE SMIRKING AT THEM WITH THE crystal belt around his waist but his words were directed at Pam. "I'm impressed little sister, trying to use the Guardians to get me to talk. Stazi trying to use our feelings wasn't working so you're bringing in the big guns."

"You think I want to do this?" Pam shook her head in disbelief. "I don't want any of us here doing this."

"We were always meant to be here," Flint told her impassively.

Telara could see his calm was upsetting Pam; she couldn't blame her for being upset, this was her brother.

"No, we were meant to be the best of Sanctuary," Pam fired back.

"Who told you that? Ira? Lucius? One of the leaders that no one has ever seen?" The derision in Flint's words spoke to Telara, there was something familiar in them. Flint grinned at her, making the bad feeling grow within. "She knows what I'm talking about."

Pam looked over at her then back at Flint. "Don't try to pull them into your disillusionment."

"You think I'm the one who is being deceived?" Flint's attention was back on Pam.

"You betrayed your friends and family for the person who is trying to destroy our world!" They could all hear the hurt in Pam's words but Flint didn't seem to be moved.

"You are only repeating what you have been indoctrinated to think," Flint spoke to Pam, but he kept looking over at Telara as she stood there with the others watching them closely.

"I'm speaking the truth!" Pam told him.

"Truth that was pushed down our throats since the moment we could walk," Flint told her. "There are always two sides and until you hear them both you will never know the truth."

"I don't need to hear the side of a lunatic that sends his Shadow creatures to destroy all that I love," Pam's voice rose in her frustration. They weren't going to get any answers this way, Telara could see that. Pam was too emotionally invested.

"So, why don't you tell us the Shadow Master's side?" Telara asked him, before he could get Pam going again.

Flint grinned at her. "Finally, someone who wants to hear both sides."

Telara shrugged but didn't say what was on her mind, the fact that hearing the side of the man who had her death on his mind wasn't really enticing, but she figured this was their only way to figure out why Flint betrayed them. "Didn't say that, but you said there were two sides, so tell me the side of the creature that wants to kill us."

"Who says he wants to kill you?" Flint asked as he started to walk around the edge of the water.

"Stay where you are!" Pam told him, gripping her Crim, but he only chuckled.

"What am I going to do?" He gestured to the crystal belt. "Thanks to Spencer's little toy, all it takes is one push of the button in your hand and I'll be immobilized on the ground, drool dripping from my mouth." Pam gave him a suspicious look but backed down. He looked at Telara. "You didn't answer my question, Guardian."

"I do have a name." She crossed her arms hating being addressed in such a generalized way.

He gave a shrug. "I was never introduced."

"Telara," she told him, then answered his question. "And the fact that every Guardian that has ever lived died at his hands."

"At his hands?" Flint asked her.

"The Magine is his creation, so yes!" Telara crossed her arms staring back at him.

"But yet the Guardians always attacked first," Flint countered. "On whose orders I wonder." A smile pulled at his lips when he realized his words hit their mark. "Not so black and white, is it?"

"What about the Shadows that attacked us first?" Tia stepped forward. "That was black and white."

"Can you say for sure you know who fired the first shot in this war of theirs? I say theirs because it was started long before any of us came into the picture." Flint looked over at her.

"There is no excuse going after innocents." Vanna glared at him.

"You're right." Flint nodded in agreement. "Innocents should be protected and not sent out to fight others' battles either." He looked at his sister when he said that. "Children should be able to have a childhood of playing with friends instead of being trained to fight a war they didn't start. What if none of the Guardians had ever needed to die? What if the Sanctuary was never needed? You want to know who is to blame then you look to who benefits from everything."

"Enough!" Pam interrupted Flint, who turned and looked at her.

"What's wrong, sis? Am I disrupting your little orderly world where everything has its place and no one questions anything?"

Pam frowned at him. "I'm not a mindless drone who follows orders, that is the Shadows that you fight with now."

"Ask the caretaker why the Guardians must die, about his role in this." Telara felt her body go cold when Flint looked at her while he spoke those words.

"That's crazy!" I.Q. protested.

"We live in a world where having a pint with a gnome or satyr is commonplace," Flint pointed out to them. "Something that someone else would say is crazy."

Telara stared at him silently, his words sinking in and making her feel cold.

Pam looked at her, "Don't listen to him, he is messing with your head."

Flint looked at his sister, "You know you've been lied to, that things aren't as we've been taught."

"Who's to say you aren't lying to us?" Pam countered.

"What do I gain?" Flint shrugged.

"Your freedom," she shot back.

The grin that Flint that flashed gave them all chills. "When I want my freedom, I'll have it, but you will always be prisoners. You just can't see the cage."

"This was a waste," Pam sighed with a look of defeat. "I had truly hoped that we could reason with you, help you to see reason."

"And I hoped to help you to see reason," Flint told her and then turned to the Guardians standing there. "Hoped to help you all see reason before you suffered the same fate as past Guardians. A fate that shouldn't be yours."

Telara stared back at him. That was what they were trying to prevent but somehow, she felt as if he had a deeper understanding of it.

"Let's go, Flint." Pam motioned for her brother to head back to the Summit, breaking into Telara's inner musings. On one level, Telara didn't want to end this conversation, but another level whispered Zach's warnings, she just wasn't sure which one she wanted to listen to. "This conversation is over."

The sound of Vanna's catch of breath caught their attention as they looked at her, but Vanna was staring behind them. Turning, they all gasped — the glowing tree that had illuminated the alcove was dimming and the crystal buds fell to the ground.

Pam looked at Flint, her eyes full of horror. "Flint what have you done?"

Alarms started going off all around them as they turned to see Flint grin.

"Guess it was the tree that was keeping the Shadows away."

18

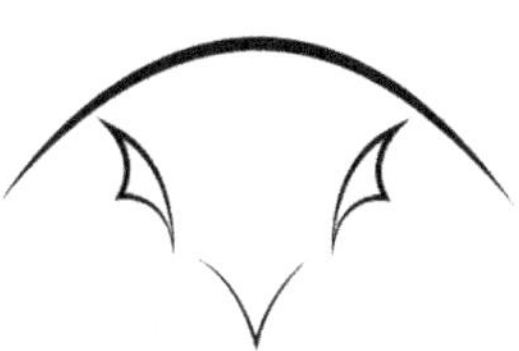

THE SHADOWS around them started to move and form into minions and other Shadow creatures that slunk from corners all around them as well as down the walls from high above.

"This isn't good." Cole pulled his necklace off that turned into his fiery nunchucks.

"Pam!" Stazi appeared in the doorway opening her mouth to say something then she looked around the alcove. "Where's Flint?"

They turned to where Flint had stood but he was gone. "He was right there," Tia said limply.

"Where did he go?" Cole looked around them.

"Forget that," Stazi told them. "The Shadows have invaded Citadel; how did they get in?"

Pam gave a look of sorrow at the darkened tree that resembled the dead ones back at the haunted house. "I'm sorry Stazi, I don't know how Flint did it. I shouldn't have brought him here."

Stazi walked into the alcove slowly staring at the tree in horror, "No..." They all looked down, feeling guilty, they had been there with him the whole time and saw nothing.

"What's this?" Vanna leaned down and picked up a black crystal that was in the water. Telara reached for it but her Rotary glowed brightly and the crystal flew from Vanna's hand to land below the now dead tree. Vanna looked at Telara with wide eyes but Telara shook her head.

"I didn't do it." She looked down at her Rotary in shock.

"Seems your Rotary doesn't like that crystal," I.Q. said as he picked up the crystal and handed it to Pam, who pocketed it.

"We'll get this to Claw." Pam looked at Stazi who nodded in agreement. Claw was the leader of the Gamma faction back in their Sanctuary and one of the top crystal experts there was in all Sanctuaries.

Stazi put her hand on Pam's shoulder. "Let's take care of the problem at hand then we will worry about the tree." Pam nodded and they hurried out of the alcove expecting to run right into the shadows they had seen forming earlier.

"Where are the Shadows?" Cole asked, twirling his nunchucks, looking around. "Where are Jeff, Spencer and Gabe? Did everyone disappear?"

"Jeff and Spencer had to get back to the heart of Citadel to get it locked down to protect the civilians," Stazi spoke, looking around. "I'm more worried about why the Shadows disappeared."

"Stazi!" Looking up, they saw Trevor coming quickly with one of the carts that squealed along the railings before stopping at the walkway leading to the Summit. "The Shadows headed straight for Citadel and the armory."

They hurried over to him all leaping into the cart as Trevor pulled a lever that started the cart moving along the rails towards the spires above the ground where they saw Shadows crawling along the outside of the buildings that hung from the ceiling. "What's going to happen to the civilians?" Vanna asked, looking worried.

"They'll be fine," Stazi told her as she stood at the front of the cart as they moved closer to the armory.

"Are they trained to fight?" Tia looked over at Stazi.

Stazi shook her head. "No, but that doesn't mean we don't have defense measures in place to protect them, like I said. Jeff and Spencer had to get them locked down before joining the battle." She looked up at the Shadows that could be seen banging on the outside of the spires, trying to get inside where they could hear faint screams inside. "There was always a chance the Shadows could infiltrate Citadel. The civilian homes were built into the stone and protection crystals were crafted into all access points." At her words, they saw a bright flash, looking up they saw a Shadow falling from the civilian spire. As they watched it plummet down it changed growing wings and flew to another spire. "The armory isn't as lucky."

"Why didn't you do that with all the buildings?" Vanna asked.

"We did, but it seems Flint found a way to circumvent those, at least he left the civilians their protections." Stazi stared intently at the Armory, where they could see Travis and his brother Jessie taking down a Shadow that was trying to get out with a black crate. The Shadow screamed out when Travis knocked out its feet with his Crim and let go of the crate when Jessie sliced down with his daggers on the arm closest to him.

"I thought the Shadows only wanted humans or magical beings?" Chance looked back at them, confused, something they all felt.

"These guys must not have gotten that memo," Trevor said as he leaped over the railing before the cart even came to a stop joining the battle with his pole blade swinging.

"I don't care what these guys are after, don't let them have anything," Stazi told them, pulling out her Crim that turned into two katana blades. The Shadows that got in her way screamed out in pain as her blades connected.

Electric bolts flew from I.Q.'s bow, lighting up the ground by Shadows who shied away from them, dropping whatever they had in their hands. Tia lifted herself up from the cart, wind whipping around her as she landed down on the ground below with her glowing whip in hand. It flew through the air, connecting with the leg of a Shadow that snuck up on Gabe. With a yank Tia pulled and the Shadow fell with a thud, startling Gabe who jerked around.

"You're welcome," Tia said, running into the armory where they could hear fighting going on inside.

Chance leapt down landing in one of the small streams where two Shadows started to advance on him. He had his flail in his hand, moving his hand so that the watery spiked ball was twirling as water flowed from the stream to the ball until it was the size of a beach ball and glowing bright. The Shadows started to back away, but Chance whipped the flail, the watery ball released after both Shadows and engulfed them both as they screamed. When the water fell harmlessly to the ground, the Shadows were no longer there.

Cole landed on the ground in a crouch, his hand flat on the ground in front of several Shadows who advanced upon him. Two of the Shadows were the humanoid minions they were used to seeing while the third one was one of the shapeshifting ones in the form of a big cat that pushed up off the ground to form a big bear like Shadow.

The minion ones could be an innocent! Telara screamed out as Vanna used their mental communication to warn Cole, her hands holding her head as the world spun around and pain pounded her temples. Vanna looked at her apologetically.

"Sorry, Telly." Telara shook her head at Vanna's apology; she could hear the remorse but it wasn't Vanna's fault. None of them knew why their mental communication was causing her these problems.

"Don't sweat it," Telara told her, breathing hard still trying to recover so she could join the battle.

Pam was in the middle of fighting a Shadow minion that kept trying to get past her and into the armory. She had heard Telara's scream and was staring back up at her with concern and suspicion.

"Watch out!" Chad shouted as he brought his icy sword down on the arm of the minion who had grabbed at Pam.

"Thanks," Pam told him and sent one last searching look at Telara and Vanna before turning back to fight with another Shadow that had taken the place of the one Chad was currently fighting.

"You okay?" Vanna asked Telara, whose face was still pale. "I'm sorry, Telly."

"It's all right Van, we need to get down there and help the others or become a liability," Telara told her as she straightened trying to ignore the sick feeling in her stomach. "We'll figure out what is going on later, for now let's keep our communication verbal."

Vanna nodded before jumping down, her belt moving to her hand, becoming a staff. She took out a minion but it rolled away before she could touch it with her staff. She narrowed her eyes at the minion who tried to scramble away. Some vines appeared from the ground, wrapping around the legs of the minion holding it still so Vanna could heal the minion. Some glowing and screams before on the ground lay an unconscious girl with matted brown hair.

Telara flipped down, trying not to wince when the jarring from her hitting the ground vibrated in her head and set the butterflies in her stomach free. She knew others were watching her closely so she did her best to look as if she didn't feel like throwing up.

"T!" She whipped around at Cole's shout, seeing the white eyes of a minion right in her face, the feeling of the clawed hands gripping her arms tightly sending sparks of pain shooting up her arms.

"No!" she shouted, lifting her arm up, her Rotary glowing brightly in the minion's face, causing it to release her arms and stumble back several feet. She threw her arm out in front of her and several glowing daggers flew out, hitting the minion, who let out screams of pain.

It turned to run, but a root appeared, wrapping itself around the legs. Telara watched as it fell forward. Vanna ran over, laying her staff down and with a glow they saw another form laying there unconscious. Another girl, but this one's brown hair was spiky.

"You okay?" Vanna looked up at her, she nodded and they ran into the armory where they saw the others fighting with the Shadows.

"Find the Liberator bombs," Stazi shouted as they moved through rooms and upstairs, watching as the Hunters fought Shadows but looked as if they were headed to a certain area, the same area the Shadows looked as if they were heading as well.

"You guys have Liberator Crims?" Vanna looked at Stazi missing the snake like Shadow that slithered up to grab her legs. Aurelius brought his pronged sword down on the Shadow snake's head, glowing so bright the snake let go of Vanna, wiggling frantically before dissipating right before them.

"Of course we do," Spencer told her from several feet in front of them, arcing his axe down on one of the big cat Shadows that was trying to sneak up on him. "I just added a twist."

Vanna frowned at him, then looked over at I.Q., who shrugged. She gave a shake of her head. "Not sure I want to know."

It was thanks to Vanna that Liberator Crims were created last year, they discovered she was able to heal the Shadows and the Shadows were fallen comrades and innocents. Then in Alaska they discovered not all Shadows are, some just disappear.

"Trust me, you do." Spencer took out another Shadow taking steps two at time trying to reach his destination. "Will cut this battle down in half."

The corridors of the armory were getting tight as they attempted to battle the Shadows, which seemed to be heading the same way as Spencer.

"You would think they know exactly where our Liberator bombs are." Jeff appeared, taking out a minion that fell over a railing, screaming.

Trevor ran up the railing as if he was a tightrope walker, taking out a snake-like Shadow that was slinking up the side of the stairwell coming after them. "Yeah, you would think they had inside information," he said, sarcastically flipping off the railing and landing on the landing, kicking open the door to the fourth floor.

"Let's not worry about their inside information, just keep them from getting the bombs," Stazi told them as they entered the fourth floor. They were standing in an open room with glass walls where they could see outside of the armory and the spires with walkways where there were more Shadows and flashes of what could only be Hunters and possibly Arions battling the Shadows with their Crims.

"Let's end this." Jeff turned and stopped as they saw a handful of Shadows already there. One resembled a troll while several others looked animalistic, which meant they must be the shapeshifting ones. "This isn't good."

Crims in hand, they advanced but before they could reach them, two let out screams as bolts of light pierced their heads, their bodies dissipating. Looking back at I.Q. he looked just as confused, his bow not even raised. Turning back, they watched as a purple blade sliced down through another shadow that dissipated like the others. There stood Paul with his scythe and Wes with his crossbow.

"Took you guys long enough." Paul smirked. Then jerked when I.Q. let loose an arrow that hit the Shadow that came out from the wall beside him. With a scream it fell back holding its head, a slice of Paul's scythe and another dissipating Shadow was gone.

"Yeah, go ahead and get cocky, creeper." Jeff chuckled. "Let's get the bombs, time to even up the numbers."

Telara moved over to the window, her head buzzing and irritating her. The last time she could remember this feeling was when her power was trying to emerge, but there was no reason for this. Ever since that stupid Shadow snake creature had almost taken her, things were off.

"Telly?" She turned to assure Tia she was all right but as she opened her mouth Tia's eyes grew wide and the world exploded around her. Glass went flying, a pain around her torso as Shadow talons gripped her in their grip and her body lifted up. She saw everyone shouting and running to the shattered window, looking up at her.

Jeff jumped out the window to grab her but a Shadow that was on the outside of the building grabbed him and she watched in horror as they fell over four stories down to the ground, where other Shadows swarmed. She couldn't even scream as others reached out to her but were pushed back when Shadows appeared, climbing through the broken window.

19

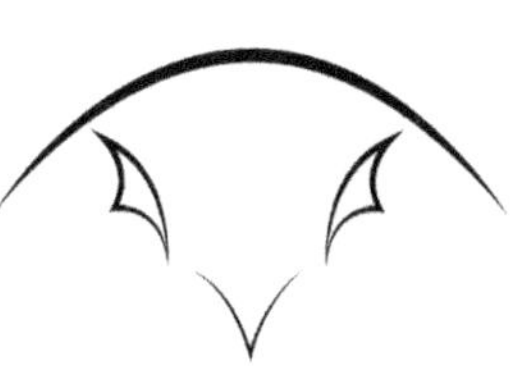

S HE COULDN'T MOVE her arm where her Rotary rested, silent. The talons were so tight around her that it hurt to breath. As they rose in the air, she saw Lucy and Jayne fighting Shadow creatures along with some other fighters. Jayne twirled a glowing rope that would wrap around a Shadow, yanking it to the ground below as it screamed in pain. Lucy would flip over a Shadow, landing in front of it hitting it in the abdomen with a baton before moving to the side and hitting it in the back of its knee bringing it down. Jayne would then wrap her rope around the neck and flip it over her and the railing.

The scene she was watching as she rose higher into the air began to dim around her as her vision seemed to darken. It felt as if the last year of her life was flashing before her eyes. Coming to Sanctuary and learning they had powers, they were the Guardians of the Sanctuary who would save the world from the darkness of the Shadow Master. And they would die doing it.

They were unlike all the Guardians before them, they had grown up outside Sanctuary and had even chosen to live outside Sanctuary after learning who they were. They made friends and worked with the Arions, they were going to defy the odds and live with the help of their friends.

She heard the sound of glass breaking once again and her body jarred as she was thrown to the floor. Groaning, she rolled over trying to raise herself up on her elbows, trying to figure out where she was. It took her a few moments for her vision to clear up. Instinctively, she reached out to her friends mentally only to scream at the pain that pierced her temples again.

"Tut tut, don't want you reaching out to your friends just yet." Looking up she saw Flint sitting on a desk, twirling a crystal rose between his thumb and forefinger. Crystal rose? That seemed so familiar; she looked around realizing she was in Stazi's office.

His words penetrated the fog in her brain, she looked up at him, her eyes wide. "You are the reason that we can't communicate mentally!" It wasn't a question. It was an accusation.

"Guilty." Flint shrugged. "Well, not me personally." He looked down at her as she tried to steady herself so she could stand and face him on equal ground. He watched her as she pulled herself up by the corner of the desk, her arms shaking with the effort.

"What did you do to me?" She hated this feeling; her body shook internally and she felt weak. Her legs were weak and felt like jelly but at least she wasn't lying on the ground.

"I just wanted a chance to talk to you without you using those Guardian powers of yours against me." Flint looked at her, that rose still in his hand. "I want to give you a chance to free yourself."

"What do you mean?" Telara slumped back into a nearby chair, no longer able to hold herself up. She put her hand to her head as a wave of dizziness overcame her. "How long will this last?"

"He doesn't want to see you die like the others," Flint told her, her head jerked up to look at him, wincing when her head spun at the action. "Be careful, we don't have much time before they realize where we are."

"What do you mean he doesn't want to see me die?" Telara stared at him. "I'm a Guardian and his goal is the death of the Guardians."

"That's what they want you to believe," Flint told her. "Don't you want to know the truth?"

She didn't know how to answer him, it felt as if he was looking through her and seeing everything. He smiled at her, as if her silence said more than her words could.

"The Shadow Master isn't the monster they're portraying him to be," Flint told her. "He is a man who had everything taken from him. He wants to end this war and, with your help, he can."

"He doesn't need my help," Telara told him. "All he needs to do is to give himself up. Then we won't have to fight and we won't have to die." Her breathing started coming easier and her vision became clearer.

"Such naive thinking," Flint gave a shake of his head. "You really think they would let him live if he gave himself up? He knows too much."

"He needs to answer for his crimes," Telara told him, her fingers tightening on the arm of her chair trying to find something to keep herself steady.

"His crimes? What about the crimes against him?" Flint shook his head at her.

"What crimes?" Telara questioned him, her hands letting go of the chair arms and gripping her hands in fists, her nails biting into her palms, the pain steadying her more.

"I don't think you are ready to hear that part yet," Flint told her, standing up and looking out the window of the office that overlooked the inside of the capital, at what she couldn't see from her seated position. He looked at her, "Can you honestly tell me Lucius has told you everything? Tell me you don't feel as if you are being lied to and I will walk away, you'll never see me again."

She opened her mouth but the words stuck in her throat. She wanted to say it, she wanted to believe it but he was right. Her lips pressed together as she shut her mouth and he nodded at her. "I didn't think so."

He looked back out the window then back at her and sighed, "But I don't think you are ready to hear the truth yet and we've run out of time." He leapt over the desk, walking towards the broken window that looked outside of the capitol, must have been the one the Shadow bird brought her through.

"Flint!" Stazi, Gabe, Pam, Tia, Vanna and Cole were the first coming through the door. Telara could hear shouting from outside the office indicating the rest of her friends weren't far behind.

Flint smiled at Stazi. "Sorry Anastazi, babe, but I can't stay, just stopped by to pick up a memento."

Stazi's eyes widened at the rose in his hand. "Seriously? You come here to take back the crystal rose you bought me?" The pain in her voice was evident, Telara turned to see Flint give a sad smile almost as if he actually regretted his actions. "Go ahead and take it, not like I ever actually meant anything to you. But you aren't leaving here."

Flint gave a sad smile. "You mean more to me than you realize." He sighed when she snorted.

"You're going back into holding, Flint," she told him, palming her katanas.

"No, I'm not," he said simply, then turned to Telara. "When you are ready for the truth, I will be there." Before they could say or do anything the room darkened as the Shadow bird reached in and grabbed him flying away.

Stazi ran to the window but he was gone as well as the Shadow bird. She turned to Telara who hadn't risen from the chair, not trusting her legs to hold her weight. "You okay?" Telara nodded. "What was he talking about?"

Telara looked up at her not even sure what to say anymore, was he lying or was he just like everyone else? "Nothing I didn't already know." She attempted to rise but Stazi put a halting hand on her shoulder, Telara looked up at her.

"Don't let him shake you, he isn't the same guy that fought by our side against the Shadows and Rogues," Stazi told her, not realizing that her words weren't as comforting as she meant them to be.

Telara nodded. "If you don't mind, I think I need to go lay down." Tia came to her aid, keeping her steady as she started to walk out of the room. She stopped and looked back. "The Shadows?"

"When we brought out the Liberator bombs, they started to disappear, we were only able to catch a handful before they disappeared along with the other Shadows."

Telara nodded at Stazi then asked the question she was afraid to ask. "Jeff?"

"Yeah?"

Telara turned towards the door where Jeff stood, looking at her with a lopsided grin, a bit bruised a little bloody but alive. "Glad to see you standing."

"Same." He nodded at her.

TELARA FOUND EVERYONE AT THE SUMMIT WHEN SHE woke up the next morning. She expected a visit from Zach last night but she woke up and no word from him. She moved hesitantly at first, but it seemed as if all the afflictions from the day before had passed. Although she was nervous about reaching out to the others through their mental link.

She hadn't talked about what Flint told her but she did let

them know that he was at fault for her ailments. Pam had felt so bad and apologized, but she told her it wasn't her fault. It wasn't, not like Pam is responsible for Flint's actions. The funny thing was, she didn't feel any malice from Flint. It was because of him that she was almost incapacitated, how could she find sympathy for him?

The damage from the battle was evident all around her as she moved across the walkways to a cart that was waiting for her with Aurelius in the driver's seat. He winked at her when she climbed in, and she gave a small smile.

The statues still stood, no damage was done to either of them, and even the Summit managed to avoid battle marks.

"So, what makes this place so special that the Shadows didn't do any damage?" Telara asked as she joined her friends, Pam, Gabe, Donny, Zeke, Chez, Stazi, Jeff and Travis.

Travis turned and looked at her. "Flint said more to you than the rest of us, why don't you tell us?" He stared at her then frowned when Lucy walked up behind him and smacked his shoulder. "Hey!"

"Behave." She shook her head at him then looked over at Telara. "We don't know why this place was spared, and sorry, but some of us are a bit on edge considering it was one of our own that caused the damage."

"And took away the protection that kept Citadel safe," Aurelius spoke as he joined them.

Pam looked guilty but Stazi shook her head. "The fault lies with Flint, period." Her tone dared anyone to argue with her but no one seemed so inclined.

Telara looked around. "Where is Vanna?" She was sure she saw her there when she first arrived.

Cole looked around. "Probably back at the tree."

"She has been trying to heal the tree," Tia explained when Telara looked confused. Telara nodded then moved to the alcove where Vanna was indeed there, her hand on the tree.

"I've been trying to heal the tree but I don't feel anything." Vanna looked up at Telara with a sad look.

Telara knelt down and put her hand on Vanna's and leaned her forehead against Vanna's. "It's going to be all right," Telara told her, though she wasn't sure if that was true. Telara's Rotary glowed brightly, the glow moving from her hand to the tree beneath Vanna's hand. As they watched, the glow expanded until the tree glowed brightly, crystal buds appearing along the branches and then bursting into crystal blooms.

Vanna looked up at Telara in shock but Telara had no explanation.

Does that mean we have two mother natures in the group now?

Telara jerked around at Chad, who had a look of regret at his mentally spoken words, but there was no pain. She started to laugh, then Vanna started and soon they were all laughing.

Stazi looked over at Pam who smiled and shook her head. "Don't ask, just join in."

20

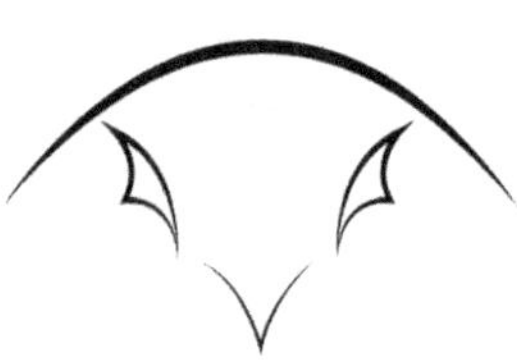

THEY WERE BACK AT SANCTUARY, sitting in their power room in their Bungalow. The room Lucius had shown them during their first trip to Sanctuary, a place for them to practice their powers and the place where I.Q. had found the stargazer. The mystical laptop that only I.Q. knew how to operate, that had entries inside as if it was a diary of sorts. The stargazer told them of the Paladins, although I.Q. was still trying to completely decipher it.

Vanna was sitting on the grass by her favorite tree with Streak, the silver squirrel that had become her constant companion in this room. Cole, Chad and Chance sat by the stream, talking about the invitation that Drago offered regarding the Crystal Paladins. Tia and I.Q. were seated in the small library off to the side.

Telara was seated cross-legged on the grass by herself; since coming back she had been silent and her friends had decided to not press her about what happened. Something she was thankful for; she wasn't sure what to think and even less sure of what to say anymore.

"HAVE THEY SAID ANYTHING?"

Lucius had been watching them from his office. They had been silent since their return. He saw the report Pam filed regarding their trip to Illinois. Nothing from the Guardians, they had refused to be part of the debriefing. Ira wasn't happy about that and was even less happy Lucius wouldn't pressure them.

"No." Lucius turned to look at Mica, who moved to stand next to him and looked down into the room.

She looked at Lucius, giving him a sympathetic look. "They are strong, caretaker, they will get through this."

Lucius nodded. "But at what cost?"

Mica had no answer to that so she stood there next to him silently as they watched over the Guardians below. She had only been back in the land of humanity for a short time but in that time, she had seen the connection Lucius had with these Guardians; she could see the hurt radiating through the man now.

Even Kull felt the pain, keeping himself distant from them, lest he show some humanity in feeling compassion for Lucius and what he was going through. Mica hoped that maybe the Guardians would come back with another Paladin, but they saw no evidence of that happening either. It seemed whatever had happened was something that caused deep reflection within the Guardians.

Lucius told both her and Kull what the report from Pam contained, hoping they might be able to shed some light on what happened at the Citadel, but they were as confused as the others. Why would the rogue let himself be captured, destroy a tree that Telara and Vanna were able to revive to let Shadows in to cause some not so minor damage and then leave, only taking a trinket he had bought his girlfriend?

It made no sense.

"I feel that what has happened is only the beginning," Mica spoke softly. "Regardless of what the prophecy says or does not say, something has been set into motion that will not be contained any longer."

"You're starting to sound like Silest," Lucius told her, to which she gave a delicate lift of her shoulder.

"I only know what I feel." She looked at him. "Speaking of Silest, has she said anything?"

Lucius gave a solemn shake of his head. "Nothing."

Mica looked at him. "What about the ones they met at the Crystal-Con? The creators of the Crystal Paladins game that seems to be more than just a game?"

"Those have me curious as well," Lucius admitted.

Mica nodded at his words, sensing that he wasn't in the mood to reveal his thoughts. "More than our family here has been affected, caretaker."

Lucius nodded at her words, his attention still on the Guardians below. The Guardians who seemed more subdued than he had ever seen.

"I hope that everyone is ready for what is sure to come."

"Me too, Mica, me too."

Pam was sitting there with Claw, Zeke, Gabe, Tobias and even Carmen in the Omega headquarters. The one place they knew they needn't worry about anyone overhearing that they didn't want to.

"The Guardians have been holed up in their home since they returned," Tobias spoke, the Omega leader reclining back in one of the comfortable chairs in his lounge. Attempting to look calm as they discussed the aftermath of the latest news.

Pam nodded.

"They weren't there when you gave the report," Carmen spoke, no censure or pomp in her voice, just concern. The leader of the Beta faction sat there looking perfect as always, but her face was creased with worry. Usually, she would be the first to belittle the Guardians or anyone who didn't hold up to her standards, which were many, but not this time. A sign if any that things weren't good.

Pam gave a slow shake of her head.

"Do ye even ken wha' thay are thinking?" Claw asked in his Scottish accent, no mockery in his voice or bright green eyes.

Again, Pam shook her head. Gabe and Zeke gave her sympathetic looks. They had been there at Citadel but even they had no answers.

"What do we do?" Pam's second, Gage, walked into the room. He had stayed back this time, his ability with the Crims returning after their time in Alaska, and he was able to go out with his team battling Shadows once again. The first year the Guardians had come to Sanctuary he had been turned into a Shadow only to be rescued but no longer able to use a Crim.

Pam looked up at him, her dark eyes meeting his light ones. "We keep on doing what we have been, we find a way to save our friends."

Gage nodded at her as did the leaders of all the factions sitting around the table. No matter how bleak it looked, they would save their friends.

Stazi sat at her desk looking at the empty pedestal that sat there, where the crystal rose once perched. The restoration of Citadel was still happening, she would join them here in a bit but right now she just needed some time to herself.

"Stazi." She looked up to see Jeff standing there. "Wes, Paul and Jayne left for home. They wanted me to tell you that if you needed them, they would be available."

"They were a great help," She said, Jeff nodded at her words. "Did you run the Analysis?" Another nod. "How did Flint shut down the defenses?"

"He didn't," Jeff told her.

Her brow furrowed at his words, "What do you mean he didn't? Our defenses don't just go down."

"They didn't just go down but Flint wasn't the one who took them down." Jeff told her.

"How do you know this?" She queried.

"Because the analysis shows that the shutdown command was initiated while Flint was in the holding cell." Stazi raised a brow at his comment. "Yes, we checked and the sensors showed that he had no access to our system while in there. This wasn't his work but he had an accomplice."

"Do we know who?" Stazi watched him but his next words had her eyes widening.

"The code used was yours." Jeff told her.

"Mine?" She felt chest tighten at his words, his nod felt like a hammer beating the nails in her casket. She took a deep breath. "Guess I will be asked to step down then."

"We both know you didn't do it," Jeff said.

"Do you think the leaders will see it that way?" She asked him. "That is very damning evidence, Jeff. I know I didn't do it but no one else has access to my commands."

"No system is hacker proof," Jeff told her. "And until we have all the information this will stay here."

"The others?"

Jeff chuckled, "Lucy has already taken care of the reports, informed them we were looking into the glitch that took down our defenses during the Shadow attack. She did send back the black crystal that Flint used to kill the tree of clarity. Figured that would keep the Leaders happy while we conducted our own investigations."

She nodded in acknowledgment, she had a great group here, the best. They would find out who used her command code and then they would find out if it was an outside force or if they had a traitor in their midst. She hoped for the former but feared it might be the latter. She didn't hear Jeff leave but she knew he had.

That rose Flint took was one he had given her so many years ago when they were just enforcers at Sanctuary in the Alpha faction. Back then he was their leader, and she, his second-in-command. They had just managed to run away the Shadows that had attacked a small mythical village that resided outside Sanctuary boundaries.

They were in one of the elven shops there when she saw the crystal rose, the only thing that hadn't been destroyed in the battle. Flint bought it for her when the shopkeeper insisted he take it in thanks. Flint put down double the amount they were asking, telling him to put it towards the repairs. She could still remember his words.

"Anastazi, you are like this rose, resilient, elegant and hard to break, just like my love for you."

Now, as she stared at the empty pedestal, she realized how right he was, for him to do what he had done, he had no love for her. It was as empty as the pedestal he left for her.

With a sweep of her hand, she sent the crystal pedestal across the room, crashing onto the floor as pieces skidded across the floor. The heels on her boots carried her out the doorway, her hands wiped away the angry and hurt tears. She was the commander of the Hunters and she had a job to do.

FLINT ENTERED THE DARK, FORBIDDING LOOKING house that sat all alone in the field. The floorboards creaked with each step he took, he watched as Shadows moved silently along the hallway into rooms and out of his way.

He made his way through the rooms until he found the sitting room that was hidden behind a set of bookshelves. There, sitting on a window seat in her cloak was the Shadow Woman that commanded the Shadows as well as the Shadow Master.

She turned with a smile. "Did you get it?"

Flint pulled out the crystal flower and handed it to her, "I hope this was worth it, I had to hurt someone I care about."

The woman took the flower then smiled up at him, "I promise you it will be worth it. He will be pleased." She looked down at the flower, her fingers tracing the petals. "Did you sow the seeds of discord with the Guardians? With the girl?"

Flint nodded. "I told her what you told me."

The woman, still staring at the flower, asked, "Do you think she was receptive?"

"The Sanctuary thrives on its secrets, it isn't hard to tell that they are already aware of that," Flint said. "I think she'll want to know the truth soon enough."

The woman looked up at him. "Just make sure when she does, she learns it from you." He nodded then turned to leave, pausing at the door. "Yes?"

Flint turned around. "When will I meet the Shadow Master?"

The woman smiled at him, "Soon. Now I would like to be alone for a while."

Flint pressed his lips together but gave a nod and walked out.

The click of the door signified he had left, the woman smiled down at the flower speaking softly, "My plans are close to finally coming together and I can't have you interfering with them, now can I Marsella?"

Deep within the crystal flower, a blonde-haired woman stared back up at the cloaked woman, hatred shining from her eyes.

ABOUT THE AUTHOR

TL Shively is an award-winning author who loves her husband and three boys; they are not only a lot of her inspiration but also her greatest supporters. She is very outnumbered in a house full of boys; even their dog is male.

Her whole life has been full of stories that used to be only in her head, entertaining her when she was younger and lived in the country where the nearest neighbor was miles down the road. It wasn't until she was much older that she finally put these stories down on paper, and it was the Sanctuary Guardian's story that came out.

She loves anything fantasy: gaming, reading, writing, knick-knacks, you name it. She loves crafting of almost any kind and comes from a very artistic family.

OTHER BOOKS BY TL SHIVELY

The Sanctuary Guardian Series

The Independence Mine Disaster

(A short story prequel in the Sanctuary Guardian Series)

The Secret Sanctuary

(Book One in the Sanctuary Guardian Series)

The Town That Time Forgot

(Book Two in the Sanctuary Guardian Series)

The Battle of Sleeping Lady

(Book Three in the Sanctuary Guardian Series)

* 9 7 8 1 9 5 2 3 2 5 0 7 6 *